WARBIRD

WARBIRD

Jennifer Maruno

Napoleon

Cover design by Emma Dolan, illustration by Jock MacRae

Le Conseil des Arts du Canada | The Canada Council for the Arts

We acknowledge the support of the Canada Council for the Arts for our publishing program. We acknowledge the financial support of the Government of Canada through the Canada Book Fund for our publishing activities.

Napoleon Publishing
an imprint of Napoleon & Company
Toronto, Ontario, Canada
www.napoleonandcompany.com

Printed in Canada
14 13 12 11 10   5 4 3 2 1

Library and Archives Canada Cataloguing in Publication

Maruno, Jennifer, date-
        Warbird / Jennifer Maruno.
ISBN 978-1-926607-11-5

        I. Title.
PS8626.A785W37 2010   jC813'.6   C2010-904974-8

for David Tyler Travis

ONE

Sillery, 1647

Marie Chouart called across the farm yard. "*Etienne, viens ici.*"

His mother sounded excited. But before he could go, he had to finish shooting his beaver. It was really a chicken, but in his mind he was Samuel de Champlain, the great Canadian explorer. Under an imaginary cap of raccoon, tail still attached, Etienne peered down his musket-shaped branch.

"Etienne," his mother called again. This time she did not sound happy.

The black mottled chicken scratched and pecked in the crusty dirt floor of the hen house. "Hold still," Etienne commanded the fowl in front of him. "Bang," he bellowed. Then he patted the small tin attached to a cord across his shoulder. This was his flask of gunpowder. He removed the pouch hanging from his belt. The chestnuts inside had the clatter and feel of bullets. Etienne leaned his musket against the wall and stashed his ammunition pouch in an empty nesting box.

As he rounded the end of the yard, he saw his mother

talking to a man in a long black robe. A great wooden cross hung around his neck.

Madame Chouart turned once more to call, this time with the face of a rain cloud.

"*Me voici, ma mère,*" Etienne said, running to her side. "Here I am."

Marie Chouart took her son by the arm and pulled him to her large white apron. Her hand pushed the straw from his golden locks, forcing him to look down at the man's feet. The Jesuit wore deerskin shoes with the design of beaded flowers.

"He is usually such an obedient child," Etienne heard her say.

The man in the black robe placed a finger beneath Etienne's chin and raised it. "You look as if you were sleeping with the chickens," he said.

Etienne found himself staring into a pair of eyes darker than the St. Lawrence River.

"Take Father Lejeune into the house," his mother directed with a nudge of her knee. "I must remove the bread." She reached for the wooden paddle, taller than his father, leaning against the stone oven.

Etienne's boots clacked across the wooden floor of their clapboard house. The Jesuit made no sound at all. Etienne pointed to the bench by the fire, then he poured water from the brown jug. The only sound the crackling of the early morning fire.

The door swung open. Etienne's father, François Chouart, smelled of earth and animals. The rolled sleeves of his linen shirt revealed strong reddened arms. Seeing

2

the Jesuit by the fire, François nodded and groped for his pipe on the mantle.

Etienne's mother entered with a basket holding several rounds of bread. "You will stay for a meal?" she asked the priest, putting the basket on the table.

"Your offer is kind," the Jesuit replied. "But preparations are underway. I must return." He rose from his chair. "A pair of hens is gift enough."

His father, filling his pipe, furrowed his brow. "Only one pair?" he asked.

Etienne knew by the tone of his father's voice that he was not pleased. Each time an expedition left Sillery, the mission petitioned his farm for supplies. No money exchanged hands.

"Your generosity overwhelms us," the priest said, rising. "But there is only room for a very small cage."

"Did you bring a cage?" asked Etienne's father, his eyes narrowing.

The Jesuit extended his palms upward and shrugged.

Giving a deep sigh, Etienne's father put down his pipe and went outside.

"You will take some bread," Marie Chouart announced, removing all but one loaf from the basket. "We have some apples left," she muttered, turning to the wooden bin by the door and lifting the lid. She filled a small burlap sack with withered apples. Then using the bone-handled iron knife, she cut a large wedge of *tourtière*, wrapped it in cloth and put it the basket.

"I will never be able to carry all of this," the Jesuit commented. "Perhaps..." he began.

But Marie knew her husband would be angry if she offered to walk back to the mission house. Last time she had returned home in a panic, frightened by an unexpected encounter with a group of Algonquins.

"Etienne is almost eleven," she said. "He will help." Her brow furrowed. "But you must keep him until morning," she said. "He is still too young to be out at night."

Father Lejeune picked up the basket and sack of apples. Etienne took the twig cage from his father. In it sat Francine, the smallest of the hens, and Samuel, a rooster the same size.

"They will be less afraid with me," Etienne told his mother, smiling at the pair of black Houdans. "Samuel," he whispered into the beard of the mottled rooster, "you will be like the great Champlain."

The Jesuit regarded the boy with interest. "You know of Champlain?"

"Of course," the boy answered. "I was named after Champlain's great friend."

"That is not true," his mother interrupted. "He was named after my uncle." She shook her head in exasperation. "He speaks of nothing but life in the wilderness."

"One day," Etienne announced, "I will go exploring." He put his arms around his mother's waist. Looking up into her face, he said, "And I will trap enough pelts to make us rich."

"You will make me proud by doing your duty to God," she said, removing his hands. "Off you go to the mission."

Etienne was always happier away from the farm. Winter had finally passed, and he had already spotted his

4

first duck. He jammed his wide-brimmed hat down onto his head and adjusted the small tin at his side. He might find something interesting to put in it. On the way back, he would walk to the edge of the bluff overlooking the St. Lawrence. The ice in the river had already begun to melt. The Algonquin might be hauling in nets of squirming silver eels. He might be able to watch canoes laden with stacks of fur heading for the great warehouses along the Mont Réal wharf.

"Do not spend all the next day at the mission," his father snapped. He had a quick temper, especially when it came to chores. "There is work to be done."

The boy and the priest trudged down the lane in the late afternoon sun. Etienne paused for a moment to lower the cage of chickens to the ground. "Are you going north too?" he asked.

"Unfortunately, I must remain here," Father Lejeune told him, putting down the bag of apples. "My duties limit me to teaching the natives that roam these forests."

The mission house lay on the road to Kebec. As they approached the stone walls, Etienne spotted a boy slumped against the wooden fence. A pair of boots tied by their laces hung around his neck. Next to him was a draw-string sack. A soft, tight-fitting cap covered his hair. Tears streaked his dirty face.

This house is always full of travellers, Etienne thought. *Everyone stops to receive the priest's blessing before their voyage to the* pays d'en haut, the northern wilderness.

Father Lejeune took the crying boy by the hand and led him inside. "Remember," the Jesuit told him, "it is a good choice. Your parents will rest in peace knowing you are doing God's work."

Etienne looked at the boy's tight, buttonless coat. Unlike Etienne's roomy woollen one, it hugged the boy as if meant for someone smaller. "Are you travelling to Mont Réal?" he asked. Etienne's parents did not like the muddy streets and noisy markets, but he did.

The boy shook his head. He gave a look of such sorrow that Etienne's heart lurched. "Sainte-Marie," he said, dropping his pack to the floor.

"Sainte-Marie," Etienne repeated. He could hardly believe his ears. This boy was travelling to the farthest mission north, in the middle of the wilderness. "How old are you?"

"What does that matter," the boy responded. He rubbed his eyes with his fists. Etienne glanced at his dark-ringed eyes.

A sullen darkness grew inside Etienne's heart and filled his chest. It was his dream to go north, to explore and live among the natives. "That's not fair," he complained.

Father Lejeune stopped to stare at him.

Etienne tried to shrug it off, but all he could think about was this boy's journey. While he slept under the stars, with the *voyageurs*, Etienne would be in his own miserable bed.

But the thought of sleeping in his bed gave Etienne an idea. If he could convince Father Lejeune to let the boy come back to the farmhouse for the night, his plan just might work.

TWO

The Switch

The next morning the mission house buzzed with activity. The voyageurs told tales of canoe races as the clerk wrote down their names.

"How did you get such a chance?" Etienne whispered wistfully.

The boy, hunched close to the fire, stared back with red-rimmed eyes. "Such a chance," he repeated in a mocking voice. "As an orphan apprentice, it is my only chance."

Etienne had to fight to keep the excitement from his voice. "You need a good night's rest, away from all this," he said. He leaned in close. "I have an idea."

"Leave me alone," the boy said, pushing Etienne away.

"Why don't you come back to my farm?" Etienne suggested, tugging at the boy's arm. "My mother is a good cook. You can sleep in my bed. I'll sleep on the floor."

"They won't let me leave the mission," the boy muttered. "I made a vow to serve God."

"It's only for the night," Etienne told him. "You can meet up with them in the morning."

Father Lejeune praised Etienne for his thoughtfulness.

He agreed to wait for the boy at the fork in the road at dawn the next day.

Etienne's socks and shirts flapped on the line as the boys approached the farm. His mother stepped away from the kitchen table to greet them, her hands covered in flour.

"*Bonjour*?" she said, cocking her head to one side, giving the boy a warm smile.

"Father Lejeune wants him to stay the night," Etienne said. "Tomorrow he travels north."

"Are your parents far away?" she asked.

The boy looked down. "They were buried at sea before we reached Kebec."

Etienne's mother uttered a small cry and pulled the boy to her in a floury embrace. Then she pushed him back, pulled off his stocking cap and ran her fingers through his hair.

"So pale, so thin, so tired," she said, clicking her tongue. "You have no family here?"

The boy's eyes glazed. "My family is the churchyard now," he said.

"He is going to the mission of Sainte-Marie, as a *donné*," Etienne explained. "He will learn a trade while helping the Fathers." He took the boy's cap from his mother's hand and the drawstring sack. He placed them on the bench beside the door. On top he tossed his small tin pouch.

His mother handed Etienne a basket. "Collect the eggs," she told Etienne. "Then the two of you have a good wash before dinner."

"It's seems strange," Etienne told the boy as they headed to the chicken coop. "You don't want to go, and I would give anything for such an adventure."

"You wouldn't like it there," the boy said. He shoved open the wooden door of the coop. "The Jesuits live among the savages."

"I know all about savages," Etienne bragged. "I've helped them fish for eels."

At dinner that night, his father hardly noticed the stranger at their table. He was too busy complaining. "I expect you to haul rocks tomorrow," he said to Etienne. "While I felled trees, you spent the day doing nothing."

The boy picked at the plate filled with *tourtière* and bread. Etienne noticed him touching his fingers to his temple. *Headache*, he thought.

"We are the same age," Etienne said to his father. "Isn't that strange?"

His father only shrugged as he chewed.

"Someone might mistake us for brothers," Etienne said to his mother.

Marie Chouart looked from one boy to the other. Both had thick yellow hair, a splash of freckles across their noses and deep blue eyes. A look of surprise flashed across her face. "*C'est vrai*," she said. She pushed the bread basket towards the boy, but he refused.

After dinner, Etienne's father smoked his pipe on the porch while his mother tended the oven. Etienne and the boy mounted the ladder to the loft. The boy removed his clothing and curled up on the straw mattress. Etienne covered him with the quilt his mother had made.

"I can hardly bear to move my eyeballs," the boy whispered, "my head is so bad."

"I don't think you should go tomorrow," Etienne said. "You should stay behind."

The boy moaned. "I must go," he said turning away. "I made a vow."

Etienne picked up the boy's clothes. *In the dark, no one will know the difference.* He pulled off his own clothes, put on the boy's and sat on the floor to wait. *At the sound of the rooster, I will be up and out the door.* The boy could work the farm with my father. The thought of the adventures that lay ahead made Etienne grin from ear to ear. He closed his eyes to imagine buckskins and beavers.

A weak crow came from the yard as the rooster readied to greet the sun. The creak of the farmhouse door startled Etienne fully awake. His father headed outside to use the latrine.

The boy groaned and flung off the quilt.

Etienne closed the wooden shutters and fastened them. He did not want the boy to wake up. He tucked the quilt about the boy's neck, and waited for him to roll over and go back to sleep.

Etienne put on the boy's coat. He raced to the bench and stuffed his hair beneath the woollen cap just as his father stepped onto the porch. Etienne turned his back, pretending to be busy with the knotted bundle his mother had left for the boy's breakfast. His father paused, yawned and grunted. Etienne grabbed the bag and ran outside with his heart racing. He got to the road just as the rooster gave the sun a full, throaty welcome.

The sky looked like the St. Lawrence River, light with snow, dark with cold. Etienne fought his fear of the eerie shadows as he made his way to the crossroads. He waited for men with torches and the laden ox-cart to pass. Father Lejeune followed in his square cap and long black cape.

Etienne joined him, keeping his head low.

At the river bank, a man in a beaver hat waited with a rifle. The strong, kelpy smell of the St Lawrence filled Etienne's nostrils. He pulled the cap down over his ears to keep out the damp.

"You the orphan?" the man asked.

Father Lejeune placed his hand on Etienne's shoulder. "He is in God's hands," he said.

A hand shoved Etienne towards the dark river. The steep path to the river was still slippery with winter runoff. In the shadows it was hard to find footing. A man stumbled, almost knocking Etienne off his feet. When the clouds parted, the sun greeted the St. Lawrence with clear, early light. Four large *canots de nord*, about twenty-five feet long, with ends shaped like crescents, were moored offshore. Behind them, almost too small to see, a small birch-bark canoe rocked at the end of a pole.

THREE
The Journey

A*lerte!*" the harsh voice belonging to the man in the beaver hat called out. Three different sizes of painted paddles, coils of ropes, oilskins and large sponges littered the ground. Short, stocky men in feathered red toques and knee-high deerskin leggings moved like ants along the shore. Some stuffed sacks with blankets, bolts of scarlet cloth and calico, then hauled them to their shoulders and waded out to the large canoes. Others followed carrying muskets, kegs of shot or bags of flour and dried peas. All worked quickly and quietly.

There was the noise of a stumble and a squawk. "Chickens?" the harsh voice questioned. "Last year it was pigs. There is no room. Leave them."

"No," Etienne cried out. "They must go. They are for the fathers at the mission."

"Then you carry them," the man with steely grey eyes thundered. He pushed the cage into Etienne's arms and shoved him towards the shore. "It's bad enough we have to take children."

Etienne took a deep breath and walked towards the

water. *Why can they not draw the vessels up to the shore? Which one do I get into?* There were four canoes in the water.

"Take off your boots," a voice said from behind. Before Etienne could tie them about his neck, his feet left the ground. "Remember to keep still," said the man carrying him. "The boat is frail. We don't need to spring a leak before setting off." He lowered Etienne into the birchbark canoe and leaped in behind him.

Etienne's seat on the sacks of supplies was not comfortable. The top edge of the canoe was less than four fingers from the water.

A second man handed him the chicken cage then hopped in behind him, making it tip.

A great circle appeared on the water and dark swells rose at each side. Etienne stared into the dark water, willing it back into calmness.

"*Allons-nous-en,*" rang out the voice of thunder.

The vessel gave a sickening lurch as they set off.

"First new moon of the season," the man who had carried him commented.

"There will be council fires tonight," the other added.

"As long as they are not councils of war," the first murmured.

"God bless you," Father Lejeune called down from the bluff. He held his wooden crucifix out to them and made the sign of the cross.

The canoe glided forward. When it met the current, it swerved. Etienne gripped the sides, his knuckles as white as his face. He hunched in the greyness as the canoe rocked, too afraid to shift. He watched the men dip and lift the dripping paddles without a sound, dreading the churning feeling in the pit of his stomach. Before long, Etienne threw his head over the side and vomited.

Wiping his mouth with the back of his hand, he noticed the chickens buried deep into their wings, asleep. Exhausted, he pulled the cap over his eyes and laid his head on the cage.

*   *   *

When he woke, Etienne found himself passing shores dense with trees. He looked back expecting to see hillsides of budding orchards, but they were gone.

"Nothing is gained by looking back," the man in the bow said. His loose-fitting shirt, open at the neck, exposed tufts of wiry black hair. He pressed his warm calloused hand into Etienne's. "I am Médard Chouart, Sieur des Groseilliers," he said.

"Chouart," Etienne repeated, staring at the man's deerskin pants and coat. They shared a family name. Etienne just knew he had voyageur blood coursing through his veins. "My name," he said, "is Etienne." But then he stopped. He dared not use his last name.

"This is Pierre." Médard said, nodding to the man in the stern. "He comes along as clerk, hoping to get rich like his uncle."

Pierre Leroux had pale green eyes. His brown hair fell in long curls about his shoulders. He wore a thin mustache over his small delicate mouth. In true French fashion, his shirt sleeves gaped to show off his expensive linen. Knots of ribbon tied his breeches at the knee. Around his waist he wore a scarlet sash. This clean-shaven, well-dressed man bore little resemblance to Groseilliers with his full beard, deerskin jacket and beaded pouch.

"How far have we travelled?" Etienne asked.

"Not far," Médard responded. "We still have a good day's journey ahead of us."

Perched between them, Etienne studied the canoe's interior. Packages and provisions balanced over poles fitted across the bottom. The two ears at the top of the cloth sacks where they were tied reminded Etienne of the litter of pigs about to arrive on the farm.

The St. Lawrence River, swollen by the melted snows, sparkled with late sunlight.

Pierre shook his long loose hair in the breeze, sending out a whiff of pomade. He turned to Etienne, smiled, and in a voice as clear as the mission bell, sang out, "*En roulant ma boule roulant, en roulant ma boule.*" Pierre's song set the rhythm for paddling. The men joined in unison, marking time with their paddles.

The little canoe bounced gently across the waves until Médard raised his arm to signal them to stop. He used his long paddle to hold the canoe still. Less than a league away, a deer moved along the edge of the woods. Etienne heard the creak of the bow as Pierre drew the notched arrow back on the string. The deer gazed directly at them, its eyes curious. The arrow flew, and the deer collapsed into the water.

Médard signalled to the men behind.

"We will have fresh meat for dinner," Pierre said gleefully as the larger canoes moved in to claim the prize.

For hours, Etienne watched the waves, the clouds, and the sky pass with little change. When Pierre stopped singing, they paddled to the sounds of the birds along the shore. One beautiful melodious song caused Etienne to seek out a bird that had black feathers like a hooded cloak over its white body. The red triangle on its chest looked like a melting heart.

Etienne passed the time naming trees of maple, poplar and beech. Just as the sun set, he spotted a tall pine, missing all of its branches, but for a small tuft at the top. "Look at that," he said as he pointed. "What a strange tree."

"Good eye," Médard responded. "That marks our camp."

The canoes passed cliffs where roots of trees clung to the rocks like claws. Rounding the bend, a pine-sheltered nook came into view directly below the tufted pine. The men saluted the strange pine and gave three cheers.

In a flash, Médard and Pierre jumped into the water and waded through the weeds.

Etienne watched them convey the goods to the grassy shore. Pierre's look told him he would not get a ride this time. With a clumsy leap, he went over the side. He whimpered as his aching legs met the icy water.

Médard and Pierre carried the canoe from the water and set it on its side. Its large painted eye stared upward to the heavens.

Soon the sweet smell of roasting venison curled about their nostrils. "*Souper!*" someone called out, and the men gathered in a circle tearing meat from the bone as fast as they could.

By the light of the noisy, crackling fire, Etienne inspected the contents of his brown sack. The largest item was a bedroll with a red woollen blanket. A stained leather apron lay inside a grey wool cloak. There was a cloth pouch that turned out to be a sewing kit. He examined the pair of scissors and spool of hemp. Opening a small tin, he found several horn buttons, three iron needles, two metal pins and a thimble. Etienne unfolded a lace-edged handkerchief of fine linen to discover an embossed silver case with a mirrored lid. Lastly he removed a soft woollen bundle. As the mound of half-finished knitting tumbled from the two wooden rods, a huge spark from the fire landed on the coarse wool. Etienne jumped up and shook it off.

"Brought your knitting, have you?" one of the voyageurs called out. His merry eyes shone in the light of the fire. A huge roar of laughter came from those around.

Etienne stuffed the items back into the sack, his face the colour of a berry. That boy's mother must have been a seamstress. What did his father do?

Before he settled beneath his canoe roof, Etienne studied the faces of his fellow travellers in the firelight. The smoke from their pipes lay above their heads like a storm cloud. Amid their tang of sweat and tobacco and loud belches, they boasted of trades and troubles. These men of the woods were nothing like what he had expected.

Neither is this journey, he thought, *bitten by bugs, scorched by the sun, and sick from the motion.*

The evening wind rustled the trees and the waves slapped against the shore.

Etienne watched a man add handfuls of dried peas to the large tin kettle hanging over the fire. As the voices died out, frogs croaked in their place.

He wrapped his arms around his huddled knees and put his head down. Loneliness burned inside him like the embers of the fire. A thickness rose in the back of his throat. He realized he had nothing of his parents or of his home but the chickens.

FOUR

Portage

"*Levez-vous, levez-vous, nos gens!*" resounded through the camp before the first glimmer of light. The long route lay up the wide St. Lawrence River to its meeting with the great northern river. In the cold, clammy air of a grey morning, they paddled upriver. Scarcely an hour had gone by when mist enveloped them. Etienne pulled out the cloak.

The water murmured as it swirled over protruding rocks. Again and again, Médard turned the canoe aside in less than a second with a single stroke of his paddle to avoid sunken rocks. From ahead came a great roar. Everyone leaped from the canoes and hauled their freight over the sides. Médard yelled above the roar. "You are in charge of all you own."

"Where are we going?" Etienne yelled back, but his voice was lost in the thunder of the rapids. He had no choice but to gather his things and plunge into the icy water.

Amable, the man in the beaver hat, tied a pack onto straps dangling from a leather collar. He slung it over his neck and pulled it up to his forehead. He turned to the man called Henri, who placed a second pack on top of the first. Amable picked up a bundle in each hand. Others did the same. They left half-running, slightly bent, up the steep path.

Those remaining threw the canoes up onto their shoulders and followed.

Etienne stumbled along carrying the chicken cage, his drawstring sack and a heavy burlap bag Médard pressed into his arms. They followed the well-trodden portage route along the gorge. The effort of clambering up the steep side of the falls made Etienne's head swim. At the top, he was breathless and soaked with spray.

But they did not rest. On they went, through deep mud, littered with fallen branches and exposed roots. Branches smacked him in the face. Clouds of black flies, thick as dust, took large chunks of skin, making his blood run.

Etienne tripped on the heavy, wet cloak, wrenched his ankle and fell into a pile of rotting branches. He dragged the cloak off and threw it to the ground. With a handful of damp grass, he wiped the blood from the cut on his leg. *Why had he let that boy trick him into this?*

When they reached the lake, and climbed back into the canoes, there was a crash of thunder, and a great wall of rain swept across them. Etienne watched the storm lash the water's surface into waves of green. His cap was plastered to his head. The cold pierced his very bones.

Médard pulled off his deerskin jacket and stuffed it into his pouch. Etienne watched the cold rain course down his bare muscular back. Médard didn't seem to notice. "*Vite*," he urged them as they paddled along the shore to the next camp.

Etienne copied the others, taking off his clothes, wringing them out and hanging them over the rocks. Naked, they unrolled blankets and bolts of cloth and laid them across the great bushes to dry. Everyone huddled about the roaring fire.

As his aching body tried to claim sleep, the bushes reminded Etienne of his socks and shirts flapping on his mother's clothesline. *That boy is probably wearing them right now,* he thought in anger. *Why didn't I bring them with me?*

*   *   *

Day after day they forged ahead. They paddled for hours before stopping to rest. Then the voyageurs laid their paddles across their laps and rested their shoulders against the freight. They passed around a common dish of pea and pork mash. How Etienne craved a slice of his mother's tourtière. The tin at his side held nothing but bits of dried peas and grain for the chickens. *Why did I leave?* he asked himself again and again, but he knew the answer.

Etienne would never forget the day his father had invited the *habitant* into their home. The man's pox-marked face, scarred nostril, and black, broken teeth had forced Etienne to leave the table. But his tales came alive as Etienne stared into the red flames of the hearth, listening. Even though the hero of every adventure was himself, the trader told tales of people who wore animal skins, danced to drums, and lived in houses built like caves.

That night, Etienne made up his mind not to become a farmer like his father. His destiny, he thought, was to be that of a great explorer like Samuel de Champlain.

They worked the canoes up the rivers and down roaring canyons. They poled across smooth water and battled frothing rapids. Each night they unloaded in the water, carried the canoes ashore, ate and slept.

Pierre taught Etienne to build a bed of pine boughs to cushion the hard earth. Even though it was spring, the nights were cold. Etienne huddled under his blanket, wishing he had not cast away the cloak in anger.

"We could always roast the fowl," one of the men suggested when they learned the last of the salt pork was gone.

Etienne threw his blanket over the chickens' cage. Afraid of crying, he tried to laugh. "You will have to answer to the Father of the Mission," he said in what he hoped would be a threatening voice. But it came out like a whine.

The twisted trees made the forest look frightening. In the distance they heard the howls of wolves. Sometimes there were rustling sounds nearby. Once, Etienne saw a pair of eyes gleaming in the dark. It would be easy for a hungry animal to take the chickens. Cringing at the thought, he prayed that no forest creature would visit their camp.

Some voyageurs settled to sleep under their blankets on the shore, while others talked in the firelight. Snippets of conversation drifted about.

"I'm planning on getting a few pelts," one of them said.

"Those natives are always warring amongst themselves," said another.

One morning, through the silver sheen of mist over the water, Etienne watched a tall bird stalk through the reeds. With lightning speed, it speared a fish and swallowed it whole.

Médard waded into the water. The heron pulled its head into a flat s-shaped loop, lifted its legs and flew off.

"There's a sign for you," Médard called to Etienne.

Etienne looked up, puzzled. "I don't know what you mean," he said.

"When you see a heron," Médard said, "it is a reminder that you don't need great, thick legs to stand firm. Even on one thin leg, you can stand tall."

Etienne gave a sunburned scowl. Stones had become boulders. Bushes were the size of trees and the water colder than he had ever known. He had trouble moving about on two feet, much less one.

They hugged the shore of the next lake and soon entered yet another river. A short, dark animal sprang from the reeds and dove into the water right in the path of their canoe.

Médard pointed at the dark head and furry back that swam a few paces ahead of the bow.

"Watch what happens when he catches our smell," he told Etienne.

The animal swam down the side of the canoe. Suddenly it dove with a great splash.

Etienne brushed drops of water from his arm. "What happened?" he asked.

Instead of replying, Médard put his finger to his lips. From around the next bend in the river came a loud sound. Etienne ducked his head under his arms.

"Sounds like a rifle, eh?" Pierre said. "That beaver is warning his family."

"The beaver?" Etienne said, looking behind them. "He made that noise?"

Médard pointed to a pile of small saplings, stripped clean of bark and branches. "He was eating there."

Etienne fixed his eyes to the shore, looking at one pile then another. Médard stood in the canoe for a moment and gazed downriver. Then he gave Pierre the signal to slow down, and they stopped where a small stream joined the river. At its mouth sat a third pile of white, shining branches.

"Time for a walk," Médard said with a smile. "You would like that, eh?"

Pierre held the canoe to shore with his long red paddle.

Médard and Etienne leapt from the canoe and walked along the brook. The soft mud soothed Etienne's aching feet.

They came to a wall of sticks woven together and plastered with mud and moss. About fifty paces long, it was as high as Etienne's shoulders. A few heavy stones paraded along the top.

"Did the natives make this?" Etienne asked in awe.

Médard shook his head. Again he put his finger to his lip. Then he lowered it and pointed.

Behind the wall of sticks lay a small shining pond. Etienne's eyes travelled across its smooth surface. Then he saw a ripple. A dark brown head like the one in the river headed towards the mound of earth in the centre of the pond. It seemed to be pushing a bundle of grass. Then the head and the bundle disappeared.

The reflection of the silver poplars in the dark surface mesmerized Etienne, and the gurgle of the stream running through small holes in the wall made him sleepy. He felt he could sit in this peaceful place forever.

Médard took Etienne's arm, indicating it was time to return.

Pierre was waiting with his rifle across his lap. Their canoe slipped back into the current. Along the river, sharp black spruce jutted from the bank. Looking up, Etienne spotted a huge square-shouldered eagle. Its snowy crown feathers drooped in long points onto its rusty black shoulders. The chickens stirred and squawked. "You are safe with me," Etienne whispered.

As they rounded a bend, they saw a great animal standing chest deep in the water. The moose raised his head at their approach and stared as streams of water poured from his face and neck. Then he turned and lumbered to the shore. Etienne heard the sounds of breaking branches as he crashed through the underbrush.

"Do all animals carry meaning?" he asked.

"You catch on quickly," Médard said with a smile. "Nature speaks to us every day, but many do not bother to pay attention."

"What does the moose tell us?" Etienne asked.

"The moose and the deer are of the same family," Médard told him. "They both mean friendship. But the moose also means a long, good life. You can travel twice as far and twice as fast after a meal of moose meat."

The four large boats carried on across the lake amid shouts of farewell.

"They are leaving us?" Etienne asked.

"Pierre and I will catch up with them at the next camp," Médard said. "First, we must take you to the priests."

Their small boat of bark followed the narrowing shoreline. Etienne watched the massive canoes become small dots upon the horizon.

"*Onywatenro*," Médard called out as he hailed another canoe in the distance. As it grew nearer, Etienne could see it was like theirs. It was painted yellow and had a large red sun on its curved bow. A man sat in the stern, steering. The woman with him adjusted the animal skin that tied a dark-haired baby to her body.

Etienne could only stare at their dark brown faces and coarse black hair. The woman's thick braids fell to her waist. Leather strings bound the ends. The man's hair hung past his shoulders. A leather band bound his forehead.

Pierre repeated these unfamiliar sounds.

"Say it," Médard insisted. "*Onywatenro*," he repeated. "It means we are friends."

Etienne mumbled the strange words as the family glided past.

They entered a small bay. A great wall of pointed stakes appeared on the hill above them and the large wooden cross of the mission of Sainte-Marie loomed above their heads.

FIVE

Arrival

The setting sun gave the weathered stakes of the palisade wall a glow of burnished silver. As the canoe moved along the river, bark shingle roofs came into view. A soldier watching from the parapet waved in their direction.

Médard and Pierre paddled down the small waterway into the very heart of the mission. *The big canoes would never have fit,* Etienne thought.

Two men and a priest hoisted the wooden bridge that lay across the canal. Etienne looked around at the squat square buildings of hand-hewn logs. Heavy wooden shutters framed windows curtained with oiled deerskins. Big chimneys of mud and stone spewed smoke. A man and boy at a saw trestle slowed their work and tipped their caps. The boy who had a wind-whipped face and tight curly hair grinned and waved. The smell of sweetgrass filled the air as they stepped onto the platform of logs.

"Welcome. I will take the chickens for you," a man in threadbare garb of black offered. "I am Father Bressani."

Etienne blinked at the ragged scar across the man's

face. "They are for Father Rageuneau," he said, moving the chickens closer to his side.

"Father Rageuneau will not expect to see anyone until you have given thanks for a safe journey," the Jesuit said. He turned to the man approaching. "Brother Douart will show you the way to the chapel."

The lay brother's long, dark hair hung in strings about dark, hollow eyes. His thick, greasy moustache needed a trim. With a toss of his muddy cape, Douart led the group of travellers towards the cluster of log buildings.

The two sides of the fort facing the forest were masonry, flanked by bastions. "Miller, blacksmith and carpenter," Douart said, naming each building they passed. He pointed to the narrow two-storey barn across the way. "Your bed," he said to Etienne, "is above the stables."

Douart led them to the threshold of a small square building which served as a chapel. "When you are finished," he told them, with a backward glance, "you will be fed."

Etienne put the chickens down next to the chapel door and followed Médard and Pierre into an earthy interior with white clay walls that smelled of warm wax. A single candle flickered at the altar, where they bowed their heads and gave thanks. Etienne turned to go, but on second thought bowed his head again. His mother deserved a special prayer. She would be the one to bear the brunt of his father's anger at his disappearance. Etienne also prayed that the orphan would stay to help his father.

His two companions led Etienne into the great hall. Eating and drinking men filled the log benches around the rough pine tables. Some looked up when Etienne paused in the doorway. Holding the chicken cage in the air, he yelled out, "I have a gift for the Father Superior."

Murmurs and laughter came from the crowd.

A full-bearded priest rose from his meal. His long-sleeved black garment covered his body from neck to feet. Around his collar of plain white he wore a chain of blue porcelain beads, ending in an iron cross. "I am the Father Superior," he said. Beckoning, the priest called, "Show me what you have brought."

Etienne carried the cage through the amused crowd. He placed it on the table in front of Father Rageuneau. "This is Francine and her husband Samuel," he said. "They have travelled far, just like Champlain himself."

The Jesuit leaned down. "Like Champlain, you say," he said, looking at the two scruffy black hens. "Thank you, we will be happy to have their eggs."

"I will take them," Douart, the scruffy lay brother said, placing his hand on the battered cage.

"You can't just throw them in the coop," Etienne protested. "They have to be put on a roost at night. Then when they wake, they'll think they've always lived there."

"Monsieur Le Coq," one of the men at the next table asked in a loud voice, "is it true?"

"It didn't happen to me," a voice replied, and a roar of laughter followed.

"What is it that you have come to do, my son," the Father Superior asked kindly.

"Explore and hunt," Etienne answered enthusiastically.

"You probably will," the Father Superior said, "but how will you serve God?"

Etienne thought of the chores he'd left behind. "I know how to raise chickens and tend a garden," he said. Then he remembered a phrase he'd heard his father say often and repeated it. "I come from a long line of farmers."

"And what long line might that be?" Father Rageuneau asked.

Etienne stared at the priest blankly. He could not remember the boy's last name.

"Your family name," the man seated beside Father Rageuneau prompted. "We want to know your father's family name."

Etienne stared at the ruddy-skinned man with black hair and brown eyes. "Hébert," he blurted suddenly, taking the name of the family at the next farm. "All the men of the Hébert family are farmers."

"Surely you are not a descendant of the great Louis Hébert," the black-haired man said, putting down his spoon. "Why, he was much more than a farmer. He was a famous apothecary."

Etienne had not heard of this particular Hébert, but he guessed by the glint in this man's eyes, it would be a good heritage to have.

"You must mean my Uncle Louis," he said, nodding. "My mother speaks of him often."

"But," Father Bressani said, "Father Lejeune wrote you were an orphan."

Etienne lowered his head, studying the black leather boots before him. "I meant my father and mother used to speak of him often," he said in a whisper.

"He will work with me," the man beside Father

Rageuneau stated. He reached across the table and shook Etienne's shoulder. "You can help out in the apothecary."

"Good," said Father Ragueneau. He leaned into Etienne and whispered, "But I must warn you, Master Gendron is very particular about work done around the hospital."

"What about the chickens?" Etienne asked, giving Francine and Samuel a tender look.

The Father Superior smiled. "You can tend to your chickens as well," he said.

"You can sleep with them if you like," Douart added, returning to his meal.

Etienne sat down to eat. The meal, nothing more than rabbit stew, tasted delicious.

After dinner, he carried his chickens with pride to the long, low building beside the palisade. "Tonight we sleep apart," he told them as he put them on a roost. "There will be no more canoes, no more rapids and no more fires."

Etienne clutched the rope handrail as he made his way up the steep ladder-like stairs of the barn. In the low-beamed loft, he paused in front of the rows of narrow plank beds to select a spot. He placed his bedroll on the empty bed directly across from the small square window. From here he would be able to see the night sky and gaze out at the moon. It was the work of a minute to throw off his jacket and stow his bag below.

Etienne opened the shutters and looked out. He caught the smell of the livestock below. To his right was the *potager*. He gazed past the cookhouse gardens into the tall pines that tapered like praying hands and smiled contentedly. He had found his way into the wilderness.

SIX

Thomas

The sound of low mumbling woke Etienne. A freckled, leathery scalp, circled with tufts of brown, shone in the light of a candle. Ambroise Broulet, the cook, knelt beside his own bed, fingering the wooden beads of his rosary. He finished his prayer but did not rise. "Give me grace," he said, staring at the ceiling, "that I not offend."

Etienne rose to his elbows. The sun was not yet up.

"Breakfast after mass," Master Broulet informed Etienne as he struggled into a worn coat. Then he bellowed at those still asleep. "The Father will soon ring the bell."

Etienne threw back his blanket, pulled on his outer clothes and hurried outside. Médard and Pierre stood in front of the cookhouse in the dim morning light.

"*Au revoir,*" Médard said, clapping a hand on Etienne's shoulder. "We leave you and your chickens in the hands of the Black Robes."

"Don't you stay for a while?" Etienne asked.

"No room," Médard replied. "All the Jesuits are coming for council this full moon."

"Will I see you again?" Etienne asked.

Pierre's face opened into a smile. "*Oui, mon petit*," he said. "We will be back."

"When?" Etienne asked.

Médard reached into his beaded bag. "Here," he said, tossing a small leather pouch to Etienne, who caught it midair. "Tonight, carve a full moon. Once you have ten, watch for us."

Etienne opened the pouch to find a small carving knife with an antler handle.

"One moon, one month," said Pierre. He undid his bright red sash. "Wear this until I return," he said, tying it about Etienne's waist. "It always brought me luck."

The two men patted him on the back and strode off.

Etienne entered the chapel, where Father Rageuneau faced the iron altar cross. Brother Douart fixed a candle to a holder sitting on a tray of sand. Father Bressani covered the pewter chalice with linen and lifted the napkin from the special bread used for communion.

The monotonous recitation of Latin and the soft thud of dropping candle wax took Etienne back to the chapel in their small village. The wooden statue of Mary, sitting in rays of dusty sunlight, always smiled despite her broken nose. Etienne would steal a glance at the strings of his mother's lace cap, but she could always tell when he was not praying. She would take his hand, unable to keep the smile from her face.

The breaking of the unleavened bread brought him back to the mission.

After a breakfast of bread and pea porridge, Father Bressani rang the iron bell that hung by the door of the great hall. A score of Huron children gathered. The Father nodded in approval as they recited their Huron prayer in unison. Then he ushered them inside.

Etienne dragged a bucket of amber water from the well into the poultry house. Champlain greeted him with a squawk and flutter, happy in his new home. Etienne scooped up a handful of meal and held it out to Francine. The hen ran to him, clucking in excitement. *She should begin to lay eggs soon,* he thought. He looked about the coop, but there was no basket to collect the eggs. After watering the animals in the barn, he set out to find Master Gendron, to whom he was to be apprenticed.

A rhythmic thumping broke the quiet of the morning as Etienne crossed the canal. When the thumping stopped, a scraping took its place. Then more thumping.

He walked curiously towards St. Joseph's, the narrow, wooden church built especially for the Huron people. The hospital and apothecary shop lay on the other sides. Etienne stopped at the large doors, peering inside to get his bearings. He glanced first at the fire pit with rows of branch racks overhead. Then, he staggered backwards in surprise when he looked up and saw a huge arched structure overhead. It was the Huron longhouse.

Rows and rows of bent saplings met at the top. Large sheets of bark, held in place by criss-crossed branches, filled in the sides. Smoke wafted from a hole, which ran the entire length of the roof. Etienne stood in awe as the smell of burning wood and roasting fish filled his nostrils.

A small naked boy pushed past a swinging doorway of bark, rubbing his eyes. Etienne watched as a long-haired woman in a sleeveless skin dress followed. She looked at Etienne but did not speak The woman emptied a basket of red berries onto a large sheet of bark and spread them about. Then she put the basket down. Taking up a thick wooden pole, she placed it into a hollow tree stump. As her arms rose and fell, she made the thumping sounds Etienne had heard earlier. The small boy held on to her fringed skirt as he stared at Etienne.

A movement caught his eye before he could see what she was pounding, and he turned to see an older boy watching him from behind a stack of bark casks. He was slightly built, and his skin was the colour of earth. He wore his shiny, straight black hair to his shoulders, parted in the middle. A woven grass cord kept it out of his eyes.

Except for a flap of cloth between his legs, all he wore was a necklace of beads.

Etienne couldn't help but stare at the long rectangular piece swaying as the boy approached. *Is this all he wears to cover his manhood?* Then he saw the pouch of cloth behind the flap.

"*Onywatenro?*" the boy said in a questioning voice.

Etienne smiled and nodded several times. He knew what it meant.

As the boy moved closer, Etienne smelled dry leaves. The boy's hair gave off a smell he couldn't name.

"Tsiko," the boy said, tapping himself on the chest.

Etienne realized the boy was telling him his name. He tapped his own chest and spoke in a shaky voice. "My name is Etienne."

The boy smiled. He ran to the woman, picked up one

of her baskets and brought it back.

Etienne peered in and saw a mound of red berries.

Tsiko nodded.

Etienne grasped a handful and stuffed them in his mouth. The warm, sweet-sour flavour that burst into his mouth surprised him. He gave a huge strawberry smile.

"Thomas," a deep, booming voice called. "Thomas, come here."

Etienne looked about to see who Master Gendron was calling.

The Huron boy smiled at the puzzlement on Etienne's face. "I have two names," he said, "and one is from your God." He tapped his chest with great pride. "My Christian name is Thomas."

SEVEN
The Grand Council

From dawn to dusk, the week of the full moon, more Jesuits arrived at the fortification.

Small bands of Huron trailed behind, clad in an odd assortment of French-style coats, skin vests and fringed breeches. The native men seemed to have dressed for the occasion.

One wore the brim of a hat, with feathers taking the place of the crown. Another wore his head shaved but for a single line of hair down the centre. Some had shaved their hair on one side, leaving the hair on the other side as long as their shoulders. Necklaces of shells, beads and claws glinted in the sun. Behind the men, women staggered beneath the weight of their bundles and baskets.

Etienne and Nicholas, the stocky young apprentice to the carpenter, were both hauling water from the well. Two men in large-brimmed, low-crowned black hats entered the gates deep in conversation.

"Who are they?" Etienne asked.

"The one with the full beard is Father Jean de Brébeuf," Nicholas replied. "He has the gift of the Huron tongue."

Etienne regarded Brébeuf's neatly trimmed hair, dark beard and piercing eyes. He was not tall, but he had a commanding presence. Father Brébeuf, seeing the boys, smiled and waved.

"Father Brébeuf is well loved in the villages," Nicholas said, drawing water from the well. "The Huron consider him a great teacher."

The priest with Father Brébeuf ignored the boys. A thin, wispy beard circled his deeply lined face. His hawk-like eyes darted from side to side.

"And the other?" asked Etienne.

"Father Mesquin has been here since the day they hung and locked the great gate for the first time," Nicolas said. "The Hurons think he is a sorcerer." He narrowed his eyes. "He looks for the devil in everything."

As the visiting Hurons made their way across the compound, they lifted their hands in greeting. Etienne and Nicholas returned their salutes.

Etienne filled his water bucket again. The boys had to haul every drop of water used in the hospital. He pushed open the wooden door of the apothecary. The air was heavy with the fragrance of dried grasses and herbs hanging from the rafters. Even though Master Gendron had bottles of castor oil, friars' balsam and sulphur on his shelves, remedies of dried bits of bark, roots and crushed leaves stood alongside them. Sacks of hickory nuts, butternuts and acorns and baskets of wizened blue and red berries sat below.

The doctor stood at a wide wooden table grinding in a small stone mortar.

"I need a basket to collect the eggs," Etienne said.

"*Onnonkwarota?*" the doctor asked with a smile.

Etienne shrugged, not understanding.

"Have you got any money?" the doctor asked. "The Hurons use fancy beadwork as money," he explained. "Our visitors are wearing lots of it to show their wealth."

"Oh," Etienne said, realizing the beads around Tsiko's neck weren't just for decoration.

He watched the doctor take a bottle from the shelf. He measured out a dram of liquid and added it to a wooden bowl. From his mortar he tipped the dry, flaky contents. Using his fingers, he mixed the two until they formed a paste. *This doctor is always crushing and stirring different leaves and berries,* Etienne thought.

"Well," the doctor said. "You'll have to make a trade."

"I haven't got anything to trade," Etienne complained.

"Not even a button?"

The word "button" jogged Etienne's memory of what lay hidden beneath his bed. Inside the brown sack was a tin of horn buttons. He filled the large iron kettle hanging from a hook over the fire. "How many buttons would it take?"

"Speak to Thomas's grandmother," Master Gendron advised. "She'll make a fair trade."

Etienne took the bucket outside to the garden. The plants used for medicine always needed water, and the more he watered, the more he had to weed. Fortunately he had a good memory. It only took a day to learn the names of the important plants and the unwanted weeds. There was a kind of rhythm to saying them. Etienne liked rhymes and the rhythmic sounds of nature. After reciting all the Latin names correctly, the doctor slapped him on the back. "It's in your blood," he said.

Returning to the well, Etienne worked his way through the crowd in the common area.

A Huron man watched from the gate. His glossy long black hair framed a face with a huge nose and full, rounded lips. He was dressed from head to toe in fringed skin garments, and his hand rested on the stone hatchet hanging from his belt. Etienne marvelled at his fierce look.

He felt a light tap on his shoulder. It was Tsiko.

"Look." He pointed to the man by the wall. "Satouta is a great hunter," he said. "He brings many furs to the village."

The man's nut-brown eyes glittered in his hardened face as he turned their way. His flat nose seemed to reach right to his lower lip. Etienne knew it was a face he would never forget.

Tsiko ran to the warrior and chattered in his own language. The warrior stood with his arms crossed, gazing straight ahead.

Etienne remembered the doctor's advice about the basket. "Can you take me to meet your grandmother?" he asked when Tsiko returned.

"You want to go now?" Tsiko asked in surprise.

"Why not?" asked Etienne. He would be able to retrieve the small silver embossed tin on the way.

"Grandmother's not in *yannonchia*," Tsiko told him with a quick short smile. "She lives in Teanaustaye, the village where Satouta lives. But it's far from here."

"Oh," Etienne said. "Why does she live there?"

"She'll never give up her heathen ways," Tsiko said. "The mission longhouse is only for Christian Hurons."

That night under the smoky rafters, the Council of Black Robes took place. Twelve Jesuits sat round the long rough wooden table as Etienne and Nicholas served bowls of stew.

Before eating, Father Rageuneau, who held the place of honour, stood up. "We will begin with prayer for the soul of Father Isaac Jogues," he said bowing his head.

"Who was Father Jogues?" Etienne asked when the boys went back to the kitchen.

"A priest that was put to death by the Iroquois," Nicholas replied in a hushed voice. "They said his prayers ruined their crops."

At the end of the prayer, Father Rageuneau spoke again. "We thank God everyone arrived without mishap: no one fell into a stream or river."

There was quiet laughter.

"Father Daniel often falls out of his canoe," Nicholas explained to Etienne as they watched and listened through the crack in the door.

Each mission gave a report. Father Rageuneau recorded everything with his quill pen.

"These hordes are never long at rest," one of the Jesuits complained. "We must follow them by lake, forest and stream. At night, my bed is the rugged earth or a bare rock."

Father Rageuneau nodded sympathetically.

"We have no means of controlling our converts," another said. "They backslide into their heathen ways."

"They should get twenty-five blows for each lapse," Father Mesquin said in a loud voice.

Etienne and Nicholas exchanged looks as the council dissolved into discussion.

"I have visited over twenty villages," Father Brébeuf began quietly.

But Father Mesquin would not let him continue. "They need to be beaten." He looked around at them all and said, "The way they beat their drums when calling up the devil is sinful."

Father Rageuneau looked up in surprise. "I believe you are being too severe." He put down his pen. "One must be careful, condemning the Huron customs."

"There has been an edict from Rome," Mesquin said. "Are we to ignore it?"

Father Rageuneau drew his hand down his beard. "We should not forbid things that are done in innocence," he said. He looked at his Jesuit brothers with troubled eyes.

"Their drums are tools of the devil," Mesquin said, rising from his seat.

"The drums should be forbidden," another Jesuit murmured in agreement.

Others nodded.

"The drums should meet the very fires of hell that they call upon," Father Mesquin thundered as he pounded the table with his fist.

"Just wait until the Huron hear about this," Nicholas said as he latched the door. Then he stopped and scratched his curly head. "How are they going to dance without their drums?"

EIGHT

Teanaustaye

Like the Jesuits, Etienne rose before sunrise and dressed in the dark. After mass, he went about his duties. The days at the mission soon became like those on the farm. He hauled water to the troughs for the pigs and ragged goat that grazed behind the stable. He fed the chickens, watered the gardens and ran errands for the fathers.

Tsiko watched Etienne work, never offering to help. "Hunting and fishing is men's work," Tsiko told him firmly. "Carrying water and gardening is work for women." He also told Etienne his chickens were not real birds because they had nothing to say. When Tsiko listened to the birds of the forest, he understood what they said.

When Etienne entered the apothecary, Master Gendron held up a hairy, yellowish root. "This," he said to Etienne, "lurks somewhere in the cool earth of the forest floor."

"What is it?" Etienne asked.

"Golden root," he said. "You make tea with this root, a cure for many ailments." He rattled what remained of his supply in the basket. "I need to visit the Huron village,

Teanaustaye, for some more," he announced.

Etienne grinned. "May I come along?"

"It will be a good long journey," the doctor said. "Teanaustaye is at least five leagues away."

To the tin of horn buttons, Etienne added an iron needle, the two metal pins and the thimble. He hoped it would be enough for a trade.

*   *   *

Tsiko, Etienne and the doctor left their canoe on the grassy river bank beside the drying fish nets. They followed a narrow path along a small stream. The trail led them through a thicket of pine and sumac. The sun filtered through the branches, making the light dance in front of them. The squirrels chattered and scolded as they passed.

Soon the trees closed in, cutting off the sky. Hearing the sound of a breaking branch, Etienne looked up. Within this cool green tunnel, a squirrel leaped from tree to tree.

Tsiko removed an arrow from his quiver. Following the animal with his bow, he waited for its next leap. With one shot he brought it down.

"Good for cloak," he said, picking it up by its tail and tying it to his waist.

The three climbed upward across lichen-encrusted granite. Small trees and tufts of grass sprang from rocky pockets. Etienne paused at the edge of a mossy outcrop surrounded by leagues of wilderness. Beyond ancient pines that stood like feathers, a small lake sparkled in the sunlight. Other than the scream of a jay, silence surrounded them.

It was a peaceful silence, not the disapproving, unhappy silence of his father.

The clean, green smell filled Etienne's nostrils and the sight filled his heart with pleasure. *This must be how Champlain felt when he saw it for the first time.* If only he could share it with his mother.

They walked on to the village that sat above a fork in the stream on the highest part of the ridge. Fields peppered with rocks and tree stumps surrounded it. Several women hoed around tasselled stocks of corn, entwined with vines. Green-turning-to-gold pumpkins grew at their base.

As they drew closer, shouts of children and the yelping of dogs filled their ears. Etienne recognized the dull, thumping beat of women pounding their corn.

He was surprised to find there was no main entrance, as at the mission. The walls of this palisade folded over each other, creating a long passageway. Etienne followed Tsiko and the doctor along it into the village.

A group of girls chatted as they wove baskets of reeds. Little brown faces peered from cradleboards propped up in the shade. Naked infants crawled in the dust nearby. One woman shaped balls of clay while another punched holes into them with her fist. A third scraped the inside with a wooden paddle. The doctor stopped beside a woman scratching out a design.

"*Yanoo,*" she said, holding it up for him to see.

He took it in his hand and examined it. "A fine pot," he said and handed it back.

Etienne watched four young boys play "follow the leader" as they dipped and dove under the racks of drying fish. Their bare feet pattered towards the new group then stopped. All of them stared.

"They never see white boy before," Tsiko explained, "only the priest and doctor."

A man was molding a sheet of stitched birch bark over a shaping trough. Once again the doctor spoke their strange language. The man answered, and the doctor laughed.

"The Iroquois don't understand birch," the doctor said. "He says they use elm for their canoes, which makes them heavy and slow."

The man spoke to Tsiko, who lifted a torch from the fire close by as the man picked up a wooden bowl. Etienne watched the man pour the sticky substance from the bowl on to the bark and melt it with the torch. "You go," Tsiko said with a wave. "I'll stay to help."

Etienne followed the doctor to the largest longhouse. Animal skins stretched across circular frames resting against its walls. Fish hung head down from poles in the shade of the building. The man who was working at digging out a log nearby didn't seem to notice the powerful raw smell that made Etienne cover his nose.

From the shade, an elderly woman, her long single braid tinged with grey, watched them approach. She signalled the woman at her side to help her rise.

"This is Tsiko's grandmother," the doctor told Etienne. He gave her a small nod. "She is head of the Deer Clan."

The old woman smelled like freshly cut grass. When she spoke, her voice murmured like a stream running across pebbles. Despite her frailty, Etienne sensed her importance.

"It was a good day to come," the doctor translated as

she spoke. "Today the villagers celebrate the first cobs of corn. We have been invited to attend the feast."

The doctor spoke with the woman again then turned to Etienne. "I must deliver letters to Father Daniel before visiting the medicine man. Wait here."

Etienne drew his tin from his pocket and held it flat on the palm of his hand towards her.

The woman took the tin into her gnarled fingers and pried it open. Her eyes sparkled with interest as she poked about its contents. She gestured for Etienne to enter her dwelling.

Furs, blankets and articles of clothing scattered the platforms that ran along the inside walls of the long house. There was an odd smell in the bark house, not unpleasant, but different. Soon Etienne's nose deciphered the smells of grass, tobacco and dog.

Two children peered from one of the platforms above his head. They pointed and giggled.

Etienne looked up, smiled and waved. Weapons, clothing and skins dangled beneath the soot-coated ceiling. The vaulted roof reminded him of the chicken-roosts.

Tsiko's grandmother beckoned Etienne to a spot below one of the sleeping platforms. She kneeled and swept aside feathers and bits of fur on the cool earth floor. Her fingers hooked around the corners of a large flat lid of what appeared to be a chest, sunk into the ground. From it she removed a flat buckskin parcel. She put it to one side then lowered the small tin into the chest and closed the lid. She picked up the object, unfolded the skin and held it out.

Etienne gasped. It was a small drum with a fur-tipped stick.

The woman gestured for him to take it.

Etienne took the stick. He tapped the tight skin surface, making a light sound.

Tsiko's grandmother gestured again.

Etienne took the drum. It was as light as the bright yellow feathers hanging from it. He banged it. This time it made a deep, hollow sound.

The old woman smiled.

A young woman brushed past them and drew apart the smouldering logs of the fires down the middle of the lodge. She raked their ashes until they were smooth. Etienne's eyes smarted from the smoke.

More women entered, carrying wood. They built a large fire in the centre of the lodge.

Etienne turned when an elderly man, his mouth framed in deep seams, shouted from the doorway. His words brought all sorts of people inside. Old men and women carrying babies thronged to the lower platforms. Tsiko joined those that climbed the scaffolding.

The doctor arrived in the doorway carrying a large leather sack. He waved Etienne over to a seat on a log. Etienne re-wrapped the drum. He gestured to a lidded basket on the floor. The woman nodded. He placed the drum inside and fastened the lid.

A woman offered Etienne and the doctor bits of smoked fish on a leaf. Other women moved about the lodge carrying strings of gourd cups and buckets. They ladled a dark-coloured drink into the cups and passed it about.

"What is it?" Etienne asked, watching the doctor drink it down.

"Every clan has its own recipe," Master Gendron responded with a smile. "You must drink it," he said, "or you will insult our hosts."

Etienne gulped it down. Neither bitter nor sweet, this strange tea seemed to taste of flowers, sun and rain all at once.

The people in the lodge grunted when a man with flowing grey locks stepped in front of the fire. His nose was as sharp as the scythe Etienne's father wielded in the meadow. The wrinkles on his face criss-crossed and jumped about his face as he spoke. His gestures seemed to be telling a story of planting.

Each time the man paused, the people grunted in approval. When his story ended, the man sat on the ground in front of the fire. He pulled a drum to his lap and beat it three times.

The men around him joined in, beating their drums and chanting. Two sang at the top of their voices, keeping time with tortoise-shell rattles. Some of the men shuffled into a line and began to move. In the glow of the fire, their faces looked blank, almost expressionless.

The pounding got louder, reverberating from the walls. The sound of the drums and the flicker of the firelight entranced Etienne.

His feet found the beat. He wanted to pound out the rhythm on his new drum along with the others. Etienne's hand went to the handle of the basket. But remembering what he heard at the council from Father Mesquin, he

49

withdrew it. No one from the mission could know his own basket held a forbidden drum. He closed his eyes as his heart surged like the mighty St. Lawrence.

NINE

The Dream

Etienne's blue-eyed gaze travelled across the marsh. He rolled his breeches to his knees and stepped in. But as he made his way across the lake's slimy bottom, he slipped. His long barbed spear splashed into the water. He retrieved it with one hand. With the other he scratched the back of his neck.

Tsiko stood less than a stone's throw away. He stabbed a fish with one quick dart.

Etienne pushed his hair away from his face in exasperation. There were so many fish, he could almost walk on them. All he had to do was concentrate, but he couldn't. His hand kept wandering to the back of his neck.

"You are not doing well today," Tsiko said. "*Atsihendo*, the white fish, not even move. It is easy."

"It's not my fault," Etienne complained. "You are too close to me."

"A good hunter does not blame someone else for a missed shot," Tsiko retorted.

Etienne didn't reply. Where he scratched his arm, streaks of red appeared.

That night, before the others entered the loft, Etienne examined his body. The large patches of red were now tender to the touch. Small red dots appeared across his stomach. His lips felt puffy and his cheeks were burning. He hardly slept for the itching.

In the morning, he discovered blisters oozing yellow fluid on his forearms. While feeding the chickens, he had difficulty breathing. By the time the sun was up, the itching licked his body like flames of a fire. He staggered past the cookhouse, plunged into the canal and floated, grateful for the coolness.

Ambroise Broulet, the cook, pulled him out. Through puffy eyelids, Etienne lay on the grass watching the crowd gather.

He felt the doctor's strong arms about him. He tried to move his swollen lips, but he couldn't speak. Master Gendron laid him on one of the wooden hospital cots. When Etienne raised his hand to the itch, the doctor grabbed his wrist. "Scratching only makes it worse," he said. As he removed Etienne's wet clothes, Etienne raised his hand again to scratch. This time the doctor tied his wrists to the sides of the bed.

The doctor's gentle hands washed him from head to toe with warm water. Etienne sighed at the slather of pungent paste over his body. Damp strips of cloth went over his blisters, soothing the tingle. When the salve touched his lips, Etienne finally felt relief and slept.

Etienne dreamed of Father Mesquin standing on the steps of St. Joseph. A large fire burned in front of him as he clanged the bell.

The Huron offered the Jesuit their beaded necklaces, belts, collars and bracelets. Mesquin shook his head and rang the bell again and again. Then he raised his arms toward heaven.

Several Hurons tossed their drums into the flames.

"Not the drums," Etienne called out in his sleep, "not the drums."

One of the drums rose from the fire. Suspended in mid-air, its drumsticks pounded the skin surface. The Huron people turned and fled. The drum burst into flames which consumed Sainte-Marie.

With a shout, Etienne woke up. His drum lay hidden in the sack beneath his bed. Father Mesquin must not find it. He flung his legs from one side of the cot to the other, making his head swim.

Tsiko appeared at his side, untied his wrists and pushed his chest down. "Stay," he said. He lifted a wooden bowl from the side table and brought it to Etienne's lips. Etienne sipped at the clear, greasy fish broth, his lips no longer swollen. Then he sank back onto the bed.

"Why did you yell 'Not the drums'?" Tsiko asked.

Etienne wiped his hand across his sweaty brow. "I was dreaming," he said.

Tsiko put the bowl back on the table. "What did you see?"

"There was a great fire," Etienne said. "Sainte-Marie was on fire."

But the effort of trying to get up had made him too tired to explain any further. He shut his eyes.

The next time he woke, the doctor was at his side.

"Leaves of three," he said, "leave them be."

Etienne frowned, waiting for an explanation.

"You had the worst case of poison ivy I have seen in a long time," Master Gendron said. "Why didn't you show me this sooner?"

"Who poisoned me?" Etienne asked, his mouth gaping.

"Not who," the doctor corrected him. "Somewhere you met up with a large patch of poisonous leaves."

"The Iroquois poisoned the trees?"

"We can't blame the Iroquois this time," the doctor said. "This is the work of God himself. There are many things in nature that are not good for mankind. You have just experienced one."

Etienne looked at his legs. The patches of red were gone. He looked around for his clothes.

"We burned them for safety," the doctor said. "But, since each apprentice receives a new set of clothes at Christmas, I've arranged for yours to come earlier." He pointed to a small pile of clothes on the chair. "You can thank Master Masson for these."

Etienne examined the rough linen shirt and woollen trousers.

The breeches were the hand-me-downs of a small man. Etienne winced as the rough wool brushed his still-tender skin. He examined the stockings to find them whole. The doublet had all four buttons. Fortunately Pierre's red sash remained tied to his bed in the loft.

Once dressed, he left the hospital. The bright red sumac leaves seemed to set the forest on fire, which made him uneasy. *Maybe if I paid better attention to God,* he thought, *my dreams would not be so troubled.* He went to the chapel.

Tsiko waited for him on his return. "Soo-Taie wants to talk to you," he said.

"I can't talk to your mother," Etienne protested. "I don't know your language."

"You can talk through my tongue," Tsiko said, turning towards the cornfields.

Etienne followed him to the fields outside the walls. The women were plucking ripe ears of corn from stalks, entwined with beans. Orange pumpkins sat at their base. The sight of pumpkins made him hunger for one of his mother's fresh baked pumpkin loaves.

Soo-Taie stopped working. She set her legs apart and folded her arms. Her dark brown hawk-like eyes met Etienne's. Facing this tall, lean woman with high cheekbones and angular features, he had trouble finding his voice.

Tsiko prodded him to speak. "Tell Soo-Taie your dream," he said.

"There was a great fire," Etienne began as the boy at his side translated.

Soo-Taie nodded, encouraging him to continue.

"All the drums went into the fire," he continued.

Soo-Taie spoke words to Tsiko, who turned to Etienne. "Who put the drums into the fire?"

"Your people," he said. "They threw in their rattles and some kind of decorated sticks."

Tsiko translated with wide eyes, hearing these details for the first time.

Etienne decided not to tell them about the drum that beat by itself. "The flames of the fire spread to the mission," he said. "Then I woke up."

Soo-Taie said nothing at first. Then she waved her hands in the air. "Go," she said.

"Soo-Taie is not my mother," Tsiko said as they left the fields. He led Etienne behind the church. In the small stone-rimmed cemetery, he pointed to a plain wooden cross. "There is my mother."

Etienne tugged some of the weeds away to get a better look. "What was her name?"

Tsiko held up his hands in protest. "I won't say her name," he whispered. "If she hears, she'll try to come back." He pulled Etienne away. "Leave her in the land of sun."

TEN

Hawendio

The warm autumn weather came to an abrupt end, and the days grew rainy. A thick fog arrived, which settled in for days. People moved about the mission like ghosts, looming then disappearing. Voices seemed to come from everywhere and nowhere at once.

Winter's approach brought new chores like cleaning out stable muck and putting down fresh hay. The animals' hair grew thicker. Etienne's wool coat felt as thin as the pages of the Jesuit's bibles. The moment he stepped outside, his teeth chattered.

In the days that followed, fur-clad Hurons filled the longhouse. After mass, they attended lessons of religion and the French way of life in the great hall. Afterwards, they did as they pleased.

One day Tsiko appeared at the apothecary shop followed by a black and white dog. He wore deerskin leg coverings, attached to his waist by a belt. His sleeves of fur fastened with strings across the front and back of his chest.

"Today we learned a song about God's baby," he said, breaking the silence. Etienne and the doctor had been working side-by-side the whole morning without speaking. It was like that with his father as well, Etienne remembered, but not as comfortable.

"Do you mean the Christ Child?" Etienne asked. "I know that story."

"How you know the story?" Tsiko demanded, "You're not Huron."

"My mother taught me," Etienne responded. It was his mother's favourite part of the Bible. On Christmas morning his father read the passages out loud. Then his mother would tell Etienne all about Christmas in the great cities of France. "And she brought forth her firstborn Son, and wrapped Him in swaddling cloths, and laid Him in a manger because there was no room for them in the inn."

"That's not right," Tsiko said, shaking his head. "God's baby was born in lodge of broken bark." He put his hands out in a gesture of puzzlement.

"Do you know the whole of it?" the doctor asked Etienne, putting down his pestle.

Etienne nodded. "Now there were in the same country shepherds living out in the fields, keeping watch over their flock by night. And behold, an angel of the Lord stood before them, and the glory of the Lord shone around them."

"That's not right," Tsiko insisted. "*Hawendio* sent brave hunters to visit the baby. They brought him pelts of fox and beaver."

"It sounds like the same story," Etienne said. He had never heard a different version of the First Christmas but guessed that the details probably didn't matter. He would not dare say that out loud after he saw Father Mesquin slam the Huron children's fingers with a Bible for not showing suitable reverence. Some he made kneel in the corner repeating prayers for hours on end.

"It's not the same," Tsiko argued, crossing his arms.

"Think about it," Etienne said. "My God is your *Oki*."

"Now you have *Oki?*" Tsiko asked, his voice rising in surprise. "You're not Huron," he said, stomping. He tapped himself on the chest with pride. "My grandfather brought his canoe when it was time," he said. "We paddled across the biggest lake of all." He lowered his voice and sat down on the floor. "Grandfather built a platform with cedar bows on the top. He told me to stay on the platform, sleep and not to open my eyes, no matter what happened."

While Tsiko spoke, the sun moved to the horizon, making the sky pink. In his mind's eye, Etienne could see Tsiko mounting the scaffold.

"I saw the flames of my grandfather's fire across the water before I fell asleep. The scratching of great claws on the platform woke me, but I remembered not to open my eyes."

Tsiko wiggled his fingers at his ankles. "I felt something feathery at my feet. It moved up my legs to my body. It stopped." He widened his eyes and said, "I felt hot breath with the smell of skunk."

Etienne caught his breath. "What happened?"

"I saw huge owl with yellow eyes and tufts of feathers like ears," Tsiko continued. "I knew it was going to snap off my head like a squirrel." His eyes roamed the room as if the owl were about to fly by. "I rolled out from under his great clawed toes and fell to the ground. I hid in the bushes until morning."

"You said you weren't supposed to open your eyes," Etienne said.

Tsiko mimicked paddling a canoe. "Grandfather came. I told him I saw a great owl."

"What did your grandfather say?" the doctor asked.

Tsiko spoke in a small voice. "Grandfather said I was not supposed to look."

"But you did," Etienne insisted. "Wasn't that cheating?"

Tsiko just shrugged. "My grandfather said the horned owl is a very great, powerful *Oki*." He brushed imaginary dirt from his shoulders. "I will get some of his power, but not all."

He dropped back down to the floor and crossed his legs. "Now," he said, patting the wooden planks for Etienne to sit. "You tell me your story of how you found your *Oki*."

"I can't," Etienne stuttered. "I've never seen God."

"See," Tsiko said. "You said my *Oki* and your God is the same." He gave a loud sniff and raised his eyes to the ceiling. "Good thing your mother *yaronhiaye*," he said. "My mother can teach her the right story."

Etienne had to turn to one side. The thought of his mother in heaven disturbed him. But in order to get any news of her, he would have to confess his deceit.

"One day Father Superior will make me chief hunter for Sainte-Marie," Tsiko said, gazing at the long-barrelled musket standing in the corner by the chimney. Etienne knew the inside was just as shiny as the outside. The doctor oiled and rubbed it regularly. "You want to hunt?"

"Yes," said Etienne, "I want to go hunting."

Tsiko walked over to the powder horn hanging on the wall beside it. "Bring your gun."

Etienne looked at him with furrowed brows. "I don't have a gun."

"You're not baptized?" Tsiko turned and asked in astonishment.

"Of course I am baptized," Etienne stammered, looking at the doctor. "Why?"

"You can get a gun, quick," Tsiko replied. "Everyone knows Black Robes only give guns to people with water on their heads."

Etienne realized a rifle would be much more useful than the drum hidden below his bed. He would speak to one of the soldiers about making a trade. But the doctor must have guessed his thoughts.

"A musket will cost you much more than your small collection of trinkets," he said. "You will need a stack of pelts."

The next morning a small drift of snow half-buried the refectory doorway. The surface of the water in the well was ice. Nicholas broke it with his fist and grimaced. "When it freezes over," he said, "we will have to go to the river."

Tsiko waited for Etienne outside the chicken house. He wore two large wooden shapes netted with deer hide on his feet. "For you," Tsiko said, shoving a pair of the shapes and skin shoes at Etienne. "You'll need them for the beaver hunt."

Etienne removed his stiff, cracked leather boots. He slid his feet into the rabbit-lined shoes. They felt light and were much easier to wear than the cold, hard leather. He pulled the thick laces of the *raquettes* up around his ankles and tied them tightly. But when he walked, he waddled.

Laughter broke out all around.

"Run lightly," Father Bressani advised as he closed the door of the chapel.

"Keep your toes pointed up," a soldier called down from his post. Etienne smiled at the little icicles clinging to his beard. "And drag your heels," he added.

Etienne struggled to walk. He fell several times before making it to the main gate. There, he tripped and fell head first into an approaching band of warriors.

Etienne faced a pair of dark, furry boots glistening in the snow. They came to a pair of knees, where they were tied with heavily beaded laces. Satouta, huge and rangy with the smell of wolf, loomed over him.

The great warrior wore a cape of grey fur over his deerskin outfit. His square hat and elbow-length mittens matched. Those with him wore coarse red blankets, white with frost, over their skin suits.

They pushed their way past, knocking Etienne further into the snow. All of them carried quivers, but Satouta's wasn't made of bark. It was deerskin, decorated with beads. *That is a very wealthy Huron. I wonder why he bothers coming to the fort?* Etienne wondered.

ELEVEN

The Beaver Hunt

The winter days died early as the sun appeared briefly high in the sky before making its way across to the west. Overhead, the trees groaned and scraped together. A thunderous, ear-splitting crack, followed by a loud whoosh, made Etienne stop and turn in fear.

"It's just a tree," Tsiko said with a shrug. "They always break in the cold."

Etienne lumbered through the snow that clogged the forest. Since the early hours of the morning, it had drifted steadily down. The sharp wind stung their faces and their breath smoked in the air. He was grateful for the fur vest he wore over his coat. Soo-Taie had given it to him in exchange for an iron needle and the lace-edged handkerchief.

Tsiko strode ahead, breaking the trail. In each hand he carried a pole with a chiselled end. His little dog peered out from the sack on his back.

Etienne staggered about on his snowshoes, desperate to keep up. He carried several small poles and a wooden club. It seemed they had walked for hours when Tsiko finally stopped. He opened his arms to the great vista of bare trees and snow. "Many years ago, beavers were as big as bears," he told Etienne. "They built this land by lifting mud from the lake with their tail." Then he turned and made his way across a small meadow. Etienne could hear the sound of running water.

Tsiko pointed to the rise of snow-covered branches spanning the river like a bridge. Stretched out beyond it, a great sheet of silver glittered in the sun.

The Huron boy took off his snowshoes and lowered his sack. His dog scampered over the crust of ice. "The dog can smell if the beaver are home," Tsiko said.

"It's not completely frozen," Etienne said, hesitating to step onto the icy surface. He pointed to a small mushy puddle in the middle of the pond.

"Don't worry," Tsiko said. "The beavers just make holes for air."

The dog scrambled to the top of one of the mounds in the frozen pond. His short bushy tail stood up like a brush as he gave out a fox-like yelp.

"Beaver's home," Tsiko called out as he clambered to the top of the mound. Using the chiselled pole, he made three small holes in the ice. When dark water rose, he pushed the wooden poles down into their home, blocking their underwater entranceway. "This will keep them in," he explained. "Now dig."

Using the heavy pole, Etienne tried to pierce the roof of the beaver house. He marvelled at how tightly the branches and mud held together. With the other chisel, Tsiko worked at making the hole larger. Etienne could hear the frightened mewls of the animals inside as the hole grew larger. In the first rays of light, seven pairs of bright black eyes stared up at them.

Tsiko picked up a large male by his tail and dropped it on the ice. One swift blow of his club, and it lay still. Etienne examined its tiny hand-like fore paws and large webbed hind feet.

Tsiko dragged it across the snow to get the water from its fur. "Your turn," he said.

Etienne reached in and grabbed one of the animals by the tail. "Got you," he cried out and gave it a swift blow. But the feeling of triumph soon faded. The way the animal had looked at him before it died filled him with guilt. After all, it hadn't done him any harm.

Tsiko clubbed two more. Four black-skinned oval animals now lay dead beside their home. "We won't kill them all," he said, looking over the rest. "It's important to leave some alive."

The dog yelped at a ripple of movement in the puddle of mush. A black head appeared then vanished in a circle of bubbles. "A beaver has come to breathe," Tsiko announced, striding towards it with his club.

A loud crack filled the air, but this time it wasn't a tree. Wide-eyed, Tsiko watched the fissures spread across the ice with lightning speed.

"Step back," Etienne bellowed.

But before Tsiko could make a move, he plunged downward. His elbows came to rest across the club, preventing him from sinking completely.

Etienne looked on in horror.

"Help!" Tsiko called out.

Etienne unwound Pierre's sash from his waist. He lowered himself to the ice and inched his way forward. He tossed one end of the sash towards the puddle of slush.

Tsiko missed it the first time, and the second time. On the third throw, he raised himself on the club, making the ice crack again, but he caught the fringed edge of the sash.

Etienne dragged him from the hole and across the ice.

Drenched and pierced with cold, Tsiko moaned and closed his eyes. Etienne knew he had to build a fire. Unless he warmed his friend's feet, they would freeze. He scrambled to gather dry kindling. He pawed through the snow to find a patch of tufted grass then made a pile of twigs. He tried to hurry, but his cold fingers were stiff and clumsy. Throwing off his mittens, Etienne drew his knife from its pouch. He struck the blade against a flint again and again until it made a spark. The grass smouldered, and he blew on it.

Numbness crept up his fingertips as he added more twigs. Commanding his frozen fingers to obey, he blew again, but the small smoking pile would not dance into flame. Etienne stopped for a moment to stamp his feet and clap his hands, trying to restore circulation.

The blue sky turned navy as the sun moved behind the trees. Etienne looked to the sky. "Help," he cried out. He looked at Tsiko. He did not want his friend to die in the dark beside a beaver pond. "*Hawendio*," he called out. "Help me."

Etienne forced his fingers to cup and blew again. This

time there was a flame. Against the darkening sky, he fed the small fire with branches. He dragged Tsiko close to the fire. His clothes were stiff, every touch crackling with ice. He smacked and rubbed his friend's legs. All the while a prickling sensation grew up the back of his neck. Someone was near. The dog barked excitedly.

He knew he wouldn't hear the footfalls coming from the forest. He prayed it wasn't Iroquois. He didn't even bother to look up until the shadows across the snow surrounded him. It was the warrior Satouta and his band.

Satouta barked a few words. Two men lifted Tsiko and headed back into the forest.

"He needs to stay by the fire," Etienne yelled. "He needs to stay warm."

Satouta reached down and pulled Etienne along. "Come," he said. Grabbing the snowshoes and the sash, Etienne had no choice but to go along, followed by the little dog.

When they finally stopped, all he could make out was a giant mound of snow. One of the warriors pushed aside a snow-covered bough to reveal a shelter filled with the fragrance of cedar. Etienne followed the men inside

Satouta stripped Tsiko of his frozen boots and deerskin leggings. He wrapped the boy tightly in a fur, and the men massaged the boy's legs then covered him with more furs.

"Lie down," Satouta told the dog. It settled on top of Tsiko's legs.

With a stir of the ashes, the fire sprang into flames, and the small enclosure grew warm. Etienne pulled up the furs and closed his eyes. In moments, he, too, was asleep.

Etienne awoke to Tsiko struggling into his deerskin trousers. Seeing Etienne's eyes open, Tsiko spoke. "I was wrong when I said you are not Huron," he said. "You built a good camp."

Etienne looked at the frame of poles lashed together. Pine boughs filled a one-sided roof that slanted to the ground. The fire in front made it a very comfortable dwelling.

"I didn't," Etienne said. "I prayed to *Hawendio*. He sent strong warriors to bring us here." He studied Tsiko's face for a reaction as he told him about Satouta and the other men.

Tsiko nodded. It seemed reasonable to him. "What about the beaver?" he asked.

"We'll get them now," Etienne said, scrambling to his feet.

Tsiko threw his hands in the air, knowing they would probably be gone, then taking his snowshoes from the side of the shelter, he laced them about his legs and leapt to his feet.

TWELVE

Moccasins

The snow, unlike the rain, arrived in silence. It drifted under doors onto the wooden sills and swelled the deerskin panes. Dark red blankets, fringed with icicles, now covered the Jesuits' cloaks. The water in the well was frozen.

Everyone went about shrouded and shivering. Etienne wrapped his feet with rabbit fur and slipped into his new boots, marvelling at their warmth. These boots were not the work of the mission's shoemaker but the needle-woman of Teanaustaye. They had cost him his old pair of boots, his last iron needle and the spool of hemp.

This particular morning, the boots reminded Etienne to inspect the hooves of the pigs and goat. In the weak morning light, a frosty mist swirled about their nostrils. Their nostrils twitched at the scent of him. Etienne gave each of them a pat and spoke to them with good cheer. He knew too well what a day without a kind word was like.

As he left the stable, he saw Brother Douart sinking up to his waist in a drift. It took him several attempts to get up. Etienne smothered a smile.

"I cannot decide which is worse, the snow, the fleas or the dogs," Douart said to Father Brébeuf, who stood nearby. "Not ten priests in a hundred could bear this winter life with the savages."

"We are all instruments of God," Father Brébeuf replied, helping Douart to his feet.

To the haunting chant of the Pater Noster, Etienne followed a path through the snow to the river. The bright sun had melted some of the snow, but it only gave the drifts a tough top crust. He placed his feet with care; it was icy where water from their buckets had slopped.

Using a chisel, Etienne chipped at the ice on the river until he had enough space to dip his bucket. He stared into the black hole and thought about the fish in these very cold times. As he knelt to scoop up the icy water, arrows of cold shot up his knees.

Etienne covered the hole with snow and left the chisel beside it. Not only would he be able to find the hole again, next time it would be easier to use.

Tsiko's winter life took place beside the warm fires of the longhouse. Squash, beans and pumpkins filled the birch bark casks buried in the floor. Ears of corn decked the rafters, and large kettles of fish simmered. There were no set times for meals. Everyone ate when hungry.

At night, Etienne went to the longhouse to visit with Tsiko, to listen to the men's stories and to watch the women make clothes. He grew accustomed to the smells of rotting flesh and tanning hides.

Kneeling on the ground, the women pushed long, sharp bones across a damp hide. Over and over they scraped to soften the skins. Then they stitched the hides together.

One morning, after exchanging greetings with the French sentries in the guardhouse, Etienne wondered why they continued to patrol the rampart.

"Master Gendron," he asked as he entered, "why do the soldiers still watch?"

At first the doctor did not answer.

"The rivers are frozen," Etienne continued. "They cannot be watching for canoes."

The doctor put down his mortar and pestle. "There is never a time when we are free from the danger of the Iroquois," he said. He stared into the contents of his mixture and paused. Then he frowned and stared off into the distance.

Etienne moved to the fire and stirred the flames without speaking. He did not want to interrupt Master Gendron's thoughts.

"I was in Trois Rivières," the doctor said in a low voice, "during the epidemic."

Etienne held his breath. Nicholas had told him that the first doctor hadn't even made it to the mission. The Iroquois had captured him en route.

"Suddenly they were everywhere, yelping and leaping about like devils." The doctor looked at the doorway. "Two stopped at my door. One carried a flaming torch."

Etienne followed the doctor's gaze. He could picture the warriors as Master Gendron described them. Their bodies shone with grease. Bands of blue and white streaked their faces. His heart filled with fear.

"The one with the torch touched the wood pile inside

71

the door, and it burst into flames," said the doctor. "The other was advancing when two shots rang out, and they both lay dead at my feet."

"Then what happened?"

Master Gendron looked at Etienne in surprise. He set about pounding his herbs with great vigour. "I left the cabin, of course," he said. "It was on fire."

That day, Etienne learned to make tea from raspberry leaves and sweeten it with a few grains from a *makuk* of rough brown sugar. There were maple trees on his family farm, and Etienne wanted to learn how to collect the sap. Then he could show his father. A smile crossed his lips. How surprised his parents would be at how well he knew his catechism. Even his reading had improved.

"Nicholas holds the Bible in front of him," Etienne said, "but he says the words differently each time."

"Not all boys are as clever as you," the doctor replied.

"The words should always be the same when you are reading," Etienne continued. "I don't think Nicholas knows how to read."

"It was not within his realm," the doctor said. "Your mother gave you an important gift when she taught you to read."

Etienne looked at the doctor with interest. He had never thought of reading as a gift. But besides the priests and the doctor, he was the only other one who could.

"Tsiko's people do not write things down," he said. "They tell everything important in story and song." He picked up the large basket of dried currants and gave it a shake. "Hi-hey, hi-hey, ho," he said, imitating them. He shook it again. "Hi-hey, hi-hey, ha."

The doctor looked up from his immense volume of parchment. Sketches of leaves, plants and flowers filled the margins. His life's work, as he called it, was the lore of medicinal plants. "Don't let Father Mesquin catch you doing that," he advised. "He won't let you visit the village if you take on the ways of the savages."

The door was flung open, admitting a wind strong enough to make the massive fire flicker. Etienne and the doctor exchanged glances. It was Father Mesquin himself.

He limped into the room and sat on a wooden chair without speaking. The doctor rose from his desk and placed a wooden basin at the father's feet. Etienne stooped to undo the priest's laces.

"Stir the fire," the Jesuit told Etienne as he eased his feet from his boots. "I don't have the flesh of your youth on my bones."

The doctor removed the Jesuit's stocking. His gnarled, bent toes had reddish blisters. Etienne poured water from the fire into the basin. Nervous at being so close, he accidentally splashed the priest's legs.

"Wipe me off," Mesquin commanded.

Etienne dabbed at the skinny white legs protruding from the black skirts.

The Jesuit lowered his swollen feet into the hot water.

"*Mal de raquette*," the doctor said as he removed a stopper from a bottle and filled his palm with crushed bits. "It's the snowshoes that cause this." He sprinkled them into the water. "There's inflammation at the ankle and the tendon that flexes the great toe."

The priest pulled his cloak up around his shoulders. "There is much work to be done," he said with a shrug.

"The pain will increase with exercise," the doctor said. "The only remedy is rest. A hot drink," he directed Etienne.

As Etienne held the cup out to the priest, he noticed how much paler Father Mesquin had become over the winter. His skin was rough and pitted. There were heavy crow's feet around his eyes. He reminded Etienne of the stone used to build the walls of fortifications.

"Well, the great warrior has agreed at last," the priest said, taking the hot drink.

"He has?" the doctor repeated in amazement.

"He will be baptized at Easter," Mesquin announced as he held out his cup for refilling. "First, he challenged me to an ordeal by fire," he said with a shake of his head. "He suggested we both walk through flames to show the people which God will protect us."

"Surely you are not thinking..." began the doctor, but the priest cut him off.

"I know all their tricks," he said. He lifted his reddened toes from the water.

"Leave them in," the doctor warned. "It's going to take some time."

"I told him I would not be spared by fire," Mesquin continued. He stirred his feet in the water and grimaced. "The Son of God was not spared on the cross."

"Then how did you convince him?" the doctor asked. "Such a great warrior must not seem to be less than a Frenchman. He needs a reason of grandeur to participate."

"And he shall have it," Mesquin said. "I promised the greatest baptismal ceremony of all time."

"Well, I can promise you," the doctor said, "if you do not wear something other than snowshoes, you will lose the very movement God gave you."

"Yes, yes, yes," Mesquin said, waving a hand in front of his face. "There are new boots for me to wear in the sack by the door." Like King Louis on the throne, he gestured to Etienne to fetch them.

The doctor slid one of the bearskin moccasins over the priest's stockinged toes. Etienne had seen boots like these before, but where? As he watched the Jesuit limp across the snow, the truth of the matter dawned on him. The great warrior the priest referred to was Satouta. Etienne shook his head. It would indeed be the greatest ceremony ever to take place.

THIRTEEN

The Baptism

Small streams of water trickled down the bare rock faces of the hills. The melting snow left islands of white amid the trees. The birch stood like bones against the dark forest floor.

Tsiko told Etienne that spring spirits brought the warmth, the birds and the greenery. The winter spirits had left, taking the ice, snow and cold winds north.

Each day, as Etienne passed the church, he heard the fine tenor voice of Father Brébeuf. Then hesitant younger voices sang out. Sometimes he heard the Jesuit and Huron voices together. Day by day, they grew stronger. Today the air resounded with song.

"You sing like a bird," Etienne told Tsiko when the practice had finished.

"I know the words in both languages," Tsiko boasted.

From the high, dense canopy, a melodious song broke out. Etienne looked up. He had heard this bird once before. Tsiko furrowed his brows and frowned. After a pause, the-out-of-sight bird once again poured his liquid notes into the air.

Etienne caught a flash of red. "What kind of bird is it?" he asked. "I can't see it."

"Never try to find the bird with the bleeding heart," Tsiko told him with a serious face. "When a warbird appears on the trail, the Iroquois are not far behind."

*   *   *

The grand baptismal ceremony was set for mid-afternoon in the Church of Saint Joseph. Every Huron in the area came to see Satouta of Teanaustaye offer himself to the white man's God. They greased their hair, painted their faces and adorned themselves with beads, feathers and fur. There were so many people in Sainte-Marie, the crowd went back to the gates. The stench of so many unwashed bodies hung in the air like fog, making Etienne's stomach churn.

Under pewter skies, the procession of priests made its way across the grassy common. The Jesuits wore white linen garments with lace-edged sleeves over their cassocks. Wooden crosses swung from the tasselled linen cords about their waists. All carried long, lit tapers.

The crowd fell quiet at their passing. Even the babies lay silent in their mother's slings.

Father Mesquin, the last in line, paused at the wooden threshold. His dark eyes raked the crowd outside. "It is the greatest gathering I have ever seen for a service," he said.

Despite this declaration, Etienne noticed the Father's look of dissatisfaction. He knew they would not follow him inside the Church of Saint Joseph. They all waited for Satouta.

A shout from the soldier on the parapet sent Etienne and Nicolas racing up the wooden ladder to watch the mission ferry approach from the rampart.

Satouta, dressed in a fringed deerskin suit, stood between the two men who poled the ferry across the water. A birch-bark casket sat at his feet. Shells and animal claws hung from his neck. His face, painted ochre and red, showed no emotion. Two eagle feathers fluttered in the breeze in the gather of long black hair behind his ear. Those in the longhouse often said he plucked the feathers from an eagle that he had called down from the sky. Everyone agreed great medicine hid in the feathers of a flying bird, much stronger than those found on the forest floor.

Satouta's eyes moved along the rampart. Etienne thought they rested on him for a small moment, but perhaps he only wished it. The famous warrior stepped from the ferry with the grace of a deer and held the casket out to Brother Douart.

When Satouta entered the church, the crowd followed.

"In the beginning, God created the heavens and the earth," Father Rageuneau pronounced. His eyes shone as he spoke, undisturbed by the gentle voice of Father Brébeuf explaining the words in Huron. "All men will die and be again brought to life," the Father Superior said. "Heaven keeps very great blessings for the good."

To this there was much nodding and grunting.

"Shout praises to the Lord, everyone on this earth," he

said. "Be joyful and sing as you worship the Lord."

Father Brébeuf closed his eyes and sang the first verse of a hymn in French. The Huron choir sang the next verse in their own language. The priests and the choir sang the third verse in harmony. To Etienne, the sound was truly holy.

Father Mesquin moved to the front of the altar. He nodded for Satouta to join him. "How do you wish to live?" he asked in a booming voice. The silence of expectation filled the church.

"I wish to live and die a Christian," Satouta responded firmly.

As soon as the sacred waters of baptism touched his body, purifying his soul according to the Christian rite, Mesquin shouted out, "You will be named Samuel."

There were murmurs and whispers.

Father Rageuneau uncovered the silver chalice of consecrated wine. With a snap he broke the flat piece of unleavened bread over the chalice. He turned to them all and murmured the Latin words of the communion.

Satouta opened his mouth. Father Rageuneau placed the bread on his tongue, and Satouta sipped from the chalice. The Father Superior wiped the chalice with the cloth and replaced it on the altar. "I rejoice to see you among God's children," he said.

Father Mesquin headed outside to the waiting crowd. Samuel-Satouta followed.

The congregation and spectators gathered around a freshly prepared fire pit. For all to hear, Father Mesquin questioned the warrior. "How do you wish to live?"

Samuel-Satouta responded, "I wish to live and die a Christian."

From his robes Father Mesquin pulled a small mirror. He held it up for all to see. A hush came over the crowd.

"Many don't know about the reflection stone," Tsiko whispered to Etienne.

"I have one," Etienne said and grinned at his friend's great surprise.

"We must live each day with the reflection of our sins, thus ever ready for our Saviour," Father Mesquin said, moving it about for all to see. Catching a beam of sunlight, he kept it steady on a small pile of brush in the fire pit. "Behold the light of God," he called out.

To everyone's amazement, a wisp of smoke emerged from the brush.

"Behold the flame of Hell," thundered Mesquin as a small flame erupted.

The crowd grunted heavily.

Mesquin returned the mirror to his robe while Brother Douart lit the surrounding logs with a torch. Father Bressani appeared at Satouta's side with the open birch-bark casket.

"Cast into the fire the charms you use for hunting," Mesquin thundered.

Samuel-Satouta lifted out ornaments of fur and bone and threw them in the fire.

Mesquin's face turned a fearsome red. "Burn your magic or burn in hell."

The warrior cast a turtle rattle and a feathered stick into the fire.

A great intake of breath came from the crowd. This time their eyes were not turned toward heaven. They stared at the flames dancing and jumping about these sacred objects.

"Cast in your drum," Mesquin demanded. "Drums confuse your devotion to God," he thundered. "They call up the Devil himself!"

With two hands Samuel-Satouta cast his drum into the fire.

Etienne could feel the wide eyes of Soo-Tai upon him. He turned to see her face register disbelief as the flames consumed the beautiful handmade instrument.

Etienne looked at Father Mesquin. His eyes were wild and his gestures elaborate. "Baptism has given you strength against unseen enemies," he announced. "But there are still people that want to make war upon you."

The crowd grunted in agreement.

"The Iroquois want to destroy you," he said as Father Rageuneau brought two shiny new muskets to his side. "I arm you against them," Mesquin said. He took the firearms and presented them to Satouta. "Go forth, Samuel," he said. "Tell your Huron people to embrace the faith which you have received."

"Name is rich present," Satouta responded. He held the rifles above his head for all to see. "But firesticks," he said, "make greater talk."

The crowd grunted and stamped their feet.

Etienne frowned. He always knew God had two voices. One was the voice of warmth, like his mother's voice when she stroked his forehead. The other was a thunderous voice, like the voice of his father when he was demanding. But at Sainte-Marie, the voice of God seemed to be a fierce, warmongering one. The more Etienne heard, the more worried he became.

FOURTEEN

Ten Moons and a Murder

Etienne ran his fingers across the small row of circles on the head post of his bed. The next full moon would make eleven. Any day, Médard and Pierre would paddle down the river.

He made his way down the ladder-like stairs without a candle. He knew the mission grounds well and could get anywhere, no matter how dark it was. As he approached the barn, someone strode towards him. Enveloped in a dark cloak, the man walked with the determination of the lay brother, Jacques Douart.

Etienne moved to the wall. He had no time to listen to Brother Douart's taunts about visiting his Huron friends. He stood as still as death, waiting for the brother to pass. Then he continued on to the longhouse.

His eyes watered in the smoke curling upward towards the roof. Groups of bronzed families were encircling the fires, cooking, eating and talking. He walked to the hearth that belonged to Tsiko's family. Soo-Taie was busy refilling their wooden bowls. Her small son drummed with dried corn cobs, their kernels now in the stew.

Men at the fire beside them shouted and slapped their legs over a game on the packed-earth floor. Etienne watched with interest as they tossed a bowl of wooden tablets that were dark on one side and light on the other. One man held the bowl while the others placed their bets. Then he struck the bowl sharply on the ground. The tablets jumped and clacked. When he dumped them out, they gathered their winnings.

"Time of sun gets longer," Tsiko told Etienne, looking up at the soot-stained roof. "Soon we will go to the sugar camp." He rubbed his belly and rolled his eyes.

All the women and children of the Christian longhouse built a spring camp in the maple grove. They tapped the trees and boiled the sap until it became syrup. They ladled the syrup into wooden troughs packed about with snow, where it hardened into sugar. Etienne desperately wanted to go along with them.

"Will you teach me *otsiketa?*" Etienne asked Soo-Taie. If he could show his parents how to make sugar, they would be able to buy something different at the trading post.

Soo-Taie looked at him and shrugged.

Etienne put out his hand, fist down, towards her. The closed hand caught Soo-Tai's interest. She put down her ladle.

"If you teach me," he said. He turned his hand over but didn't open it.

Soo-Taie took his fist into her two hands. She grunted.

Etienne opened his fingers one by one. The silver scissors sparkled in the firelight. Soo-Taie cocked her head to one side then the other.

"See," Etienne said. He put his two fingers in the scissor holes. He pulled a stray wisp of hair from the thick braid that reached her waist. The small scissors sheared right through it. He held the wisp of hair in the air, then let it fall to the floor.

Soo-Taie gasped and opened her palm. Etienne placed the scissors onto it. The bargain had been made.

*   *   *

Tsiko walked back with Etienne in the cool evening air.

A high-pitched cry coming from the other side of the palisade startled them both. Tsiko's body went taut. He raised a hand.

"Is it Iroquois?" Etienne whispered, his heart pounding in fear.

Tsiko put his finger to his lips. He went to the wall and listened. A second cry, like the yelp of a dog, made Etienne cringe. They heard a thud, followed by a groan.

Tsiko ran to the gate, unbolted it and pushed it open.

"What's going on?" yelled the soldier on duty.

A figure lay on the path. From the breeches and boots, it was clearly a Frenchman.

The guard's lantern bounced and swung as he ran towards them. His light illuminated the body. The man lay on his stomach. From beneath the cloak covering his head, a pool of dark, sticky liquid seeped into the ground.

"Ring the bell," the soldier said to Etienne. "You fetch the doctor," he told Tsiko.

Master Gendron walked about the body with his lantern aloft. Father Rageuneau and Father Bressani crossed themselves and murmured prayers. The doctor knelt and pressed his fingers to the cold, clammy neck. Then he rolled him over.

Everyone gasped at the great gaping gash across his forehead. Jacques Douart had met his death by tomahawk.

Etienne shuddered. He tried hard to keep a brave face as his throat tightened and his lips went white. All he had to do was look away, but he couldn't tear his eyes away from the ghastly sight of Brother Douart's dead body.

"He didn't receive Extreme Unction," Father Bressani whispered.

"We can never predict when we will be called to God," Father Rageuneau replied.

*   *   *

The carpenter affixed a wooden cross to the standing lid of the pine box. Nicholas planed the sides of the coffin. His face was as white as the shavings that curled and fell to the floor.

A square of grey blanket covered the single small window. After Master Gendron had washed the caked blood from Douart's scalp, he repaired the gaping wound. The only sound was the buzzing of flies. Jacques Douart's fish-belly grey skin attracted many. Etienne watched the doctor's gentle hands dress the dead man in white linen.

The shrouded corpse rested on the table in the

infirmary. The fire in the hearth lay banked almost to the point of extinction, and candles flickered in wooden stands at each corner. Father Rageuneau approached. He made the sign of the cross over the body. "May the Lord have mercy on your soul," he whispered. He crossed himself then dropped to his knees on the hard earth floor. "I ask in the name of the Lord for a place for our brother in eternity." The Jesuit, with his rosary threaded through his fingers, moved his lips in silence. Etienne had watched his mother kneel and say her beads in the very same way, every day of his life. She would kiss the little wooden cross that hung from the rosary of pearls before she rose. Etienne's eyes brimmed at the memory.

With a groan, Father Rageuneau rose. He wound the strand of blue porcelain beads around the dead man's clasped hands. Then, taking a small wooden brush from a bowl nearby, he sprinkled the body with holy water.

High Mass was to be at dusk. They would bury Brother Douart behind the church. The little cemetery behind St. Joseph would now have a Frenchman among the Christian Hurons.

As news of the murder spread, Hurons came from neighbouring villages to report that the murderers demanded that all Huron who had become Christians return to their old ways. The Jesuits were no longer to visit the Huron villages.

That night the two boys once again watched and listened from the kitchen door as the priests and brothers met.

"How will these murderers be brought to justice?" Father Daniel asked.

Father Rageuneau picked up his quill pen. "We will conform to Huron law," he said. "They will have to live with the shame of losing some of their possessions. A tribute must be paid."

Father Mesquin stood in protest. "Murder is a sin. They *must* be punished."

Father Rageuneau held up his hand. "Taking lives as punishment only leaves fatherless children. We will leave their judgment to the Almighty," he said.

Father Mesquin turned on his heel and left.

"Was it the Iroquois?" Etienne asked Nicholas in an incredulous whisper.

"No," Nicholas said with wide eyes. "It was heathen Huron."

FIFTEEN
The Gifts

The evening of the eleventh moon, a number of Hurons gathered at the main gates. Four highly-decorated warriors asked to speak with the Father Superior.

Father Brébeuf rushed to Etienne and Tsiko, his skirts swishing. "Fetch the Fathers."

The door to Father Rageuneau's room sat ajar. Etienne knocked then gave it a small push. Father Rageuneau was working in the yellow glow of a candle at a small wooden table. There was no heat. He only made use of his fireplace when the weather was bitter, in order to set an example to those he directed. Above his desk, the Saviour hung painfully from the cross.

Etienne coughed, and Father Rageuneau looked up quizzically.

"There are Huron to see you," Etienne said.

The Father Superior returned his pen to the inkwell. He closed his eyes, clasped his hands and tilted his head towards the ceiling in prayer.

In his own room, Father Mesquin sat on his wooden bench with eyes closed. His prayer book was about to fall from his hand. He woke with a start when Tsiko removed it and placed it on his table. "What are you doing in my chamber?"

"Father Brébeuf..." Tsiko said as Etienne came to his side.

"You thought it was acceptable to enter without permission?" Mesquin asked.

"The door was open," Tsiko said. "We came to tell you…" he started to say, but Father Mesquin ignored him.

"I was praying," Mesquin said to Tsiko. "Who told you you could come in?"

"But…Father Rageuneau…" stammered Tsiko

The priest adjusted his skirts, muttering about how the Indians were unable to tell the truth.

Tsiko crossed his arms angrily. "I do not lie," he said.

Etienne felt his cheeks grow hot.

The priest's eyes blazed like the hot coals of his fire as he stood up. His hand shot out from a long black sleeve. The smack against Tsiko's cheek startled Etienne. Even though he did not feel the sting, his own eyes filled with tears.

"You knock," Father Mesquin said. "If there is no answer, you come back." Then the priest sighed as if he was very, very tired and turned to Etienne. "What do you wish?

"There are Huron at the gate," Etienne said.

"There are Huron everywhere," the priest replied, pushing past them both.

Tsiko raised his chin and spoke through clenched teeth. "You do not know how to speak the truth," he said to the empty room. He turned to Etienne. "He was asleep."

The boys remained near the gate to watch. Nicholas, Ambroise Broulet, the cook, and Louie Gaubert, the blacksmith, joined him. Master Gaubert looked old enough to be Etienne's grandfather, but there was nothing frail about him. The wizened blacksmith kept Ambroise's cooking pots in good repair, which is why he got larger helpings than anyone else.

Father Rageuneau greeted the speaker of the Huron party. From his gown he drew a small bundle of sticks and handed it to the speaker.

"Why did he give the chief sticks?" Etienne asked in a whisper.

"It's the number of gifts the Hurons have to give," Louise Gaubert said. "It's the punishment for murder."

"I heard each gift is a thousand wampum beads," said Nicholas.

"They should ask for one hundred bundles of beaver skins," Ambroise Broulet replied.

"Gifts for the murder of a Huron man is thirty presents," Tsiko informed Etienne. "Ten more for the murder of a woman," he added.

"That makes sense," Etienne said with a nod. It seemed a Huron woman's work never ended. She gathered the year's supply of firewood before sowing, tilling and harvesting. She smoked fish, dressed skins, and made clothing. Every day she prepared food. Even Etienne's mother received help from his father, when he had the time.

The day for the gift giving ceremony was set. The Huron chiefs left as the sky, feathered with wisps of white, faded to dark.

*　*　*

The crowd gathered in the field in front of the Mission longhouse. Etienne, Nicholas and Tsiko were to carry the gifts to the special platform built for their display.

The Hurons presented their first gifts at the gate. Father Brébeuf made a great show of examining the twists of tobacco, leather pouches and braids of sweetgrass.

"Please enter," Father Rageuneau finally said.

The huge procession of moccasins moved past the gate into the clearing. Etienne's eyes scanned the visitors. Some men wore their hair above their ears in great rolls. Others braided it with feathers and wore it to one side. They walked in clans, wearing skins like cloaks, bodies painted, oiled and greased. Each chief carried a skin bundle, birch-bark casket or basket.

All was silent. Even the birds had stopped chirping.

"Did the people of your village come?" Etienne whispered.

"There are my uncles," Tsiko said, pointing to two men passing through the gate. Etienne recognized a hunter from the day Tsiko had fallen into the icy water. The other man wore necklaces of animal claws and bones. Tails of fur swung from his eel-skin headband. Etienne knew him to be the medicine-man of the Cord People. The doctor often conferred with him.

"So you are Cord," said Etienne.

"My father was Cord," Tsiko told him, "my mother, Deer. Uncles said I must be Cord. But Owl Oki gave me great courage. I became Deer to make my mother proud."

Etienne shot his friend a look of surprise. It would take great courage indeed to disobey those uncles. Tsiko wanted to please his mother even though she was dead. The thought that Etienne might never be able to please his mother again stabbed him like a knife.

The ceremony began when the chief of all the clans moved forward and spoke as the three boys carried the gifts to Father Brébeuf.

"Here is something by which we withdraw the tomahawk from the wound," Father Brébeuf translated for all. "This present makes it fall from avenging hands," he added.

Father Rageuneau accepted three magnificent mink skins dangling from a decorated pole.

The Huron presenting the gift grunted and moved back. Another chief moved forward.

"Here is something to wipe the blood from the wound," Brébeuf called out. The Father Superior accepted a bundle of beaver pelts.

The next gift, an ice chisel, symbolized the earth cracking at the horror of the crime.

A magnificent pair of moose hide mittens, trimmed with fur, was for placing a stone over the crack. Then the whole assembly rose. They danced to stamp the earth back into place.

Etienne, Tsiko and Nicholas joined in, despite Father Mesquin's scowl of disapproval.

The gift of matching moccasins was to help make village paths peaceful once again.

The sixth gift was a three-pound plug of tobacco for

the father of the victim. A tobacco pouch, decorated with porcupine quills, was to restore the peace of mind of the offended father.

These gifts, placed into Etienne's hands, made his father's angry face loom before him. How would he restore the peace of mind of his offended father?

Tsiko passed with an intricately carved wooden bowl. It was to hold a drink for the mother of the victim, for she would suffer and sicken at the death of her son.

Etienne pictured his mother lugging a pail of water into the kitchen. The thought of her being sick left him cold. Would his disappearance have made her ill?

A large moose skin, so heavy that it took all three boys to carry it, was a place for the mother to rest during her time of mourning.

After that, Nicholas tiredly plunked himself down on the grass, but Tsiko pulled at his arm to rise. There was more to come.

"The next gifts are to help clear the way for the journey to the sun," Father Brébeuf said, as a warrior laid a deerskin bundle at Father Rageuneau's feet.

"Brother Douart won't be leaving the cemetery," Nicholas whispered.

Tsiko shot him a stern look.

"Don't say his name," Etienne warned.

"Why not?"

"Just don't."

Father Rageuneau unfolded the bundle to reveal four knives, each one different. He carefully examined the small crooked knife, the skinning knife, the hunting knife and the snow knife. He nodded in approval.

The next warrior carried his bundle to Father Brébeuf himself. The four fox skins were to pillow the dead one's head.

As the sky faded to gunpowder grey, the wooden church melted into the shadows. The chiefs of the clans stood silent, waiting. The air filled with expectation in the torches' glare.

Father Brébeuf brought a small wooden box and placed it at the Father Superior's feet. With a wave, he dismissed the boys to the edge of the crowd.

The headmen of each clan stepped forward. Their upper bodies glistened in the light of the torches. Each presented Father Rageuneau with strings of beadwork to bring the bones of the dead man together.

Father Rageuneau stretched out his arms, and they laid their gifts across them.

Father Brébeuf opened the small wooden box. The revered Jesuit brought out a beaded belt. The chief accepted it as recognition of the restored trust between the Huron and the French. He grunted in approval and all withdrew in silence.

SIXTEEN

Teanaustaye Destroyed

Once again Etienne dreamed. This time, he was sitting at the top of a tree overlooking the land. In the middle of the forest a great fire burned. A flock of blue jays on a nearby bough called to him, then they rose and headed for the fire. Some flew around it. Others flew directly into it, but they did not burn. Their feathers turned deep blue, then purple. They became crows.

Some of the crows returned to the branch where Etienne was sitting. They folded their stiff wings, fixed him with their beady black eyes and cackled. Others surrounded Etienne in a great flurry of dark wings. They scratched at his body with their claws. Some pecked at his chest. Then the attacking crows lifted him out of the tree towards the fire. He felt the heat of the flames as they flew closer and closer. As his body turned black, Etienne lurched awake.

At first, he wasn't even sure where he was, but the cook's morning murmurs brought him back to the mission. He glanced at the rays of the rising sun through the gap in the wooden slats. *No wonder this bed was empty when*

I arrived, he thought. The buckled and broken shutters did not close properly. Etienne often debated whether his blanket would be better over the window than covering his body. *If only I had kept that woollen cloak.* Each time he thought about it, his foolishness amazed him.

That morning, Etienne and Tsiko slipped their canoe into the morning river mist. Father Bressani had commissioned them to take letters to Father Daniel at Teanaustaye.

When they entered the village, an old warrior was squatting on the ground with a group of boys. Etienne and Tsiko stopped to watch.

The man scratched two large squares in the earth. Then he made several smaller ones inside. The man passed his hand in front of one of the boys' faces. The boy closed his eyes. The man filled some of his squares with nuts and stones and grunted. The boy opened his eyes and stared at the arrangement. Then the man covered his square with a basket. The boy picked up a handful of stones and nuts and arranged them in what he hoped was the same pattern.

When the man lifted his basket, the patterns matched. He patted the boy on the shoulder.

Father Daniel approached the small group with a smile.

"Where is everyone?" Etienne asked. The village seemed exceptionally quiet.

"They've all gone off to trade," the priest replied. "Kettles and knives have become the most important things in life," he muttered, taking the package.

The boys walked past the hut of the medicine man. Turtles without tails dangled from the doorway. Etienne stared in horror at the sticky red blood draining into the gourd bowl below.

Tsiko shrugged. "Medicine man makes rattles," he explained as angry voices shattered the silence. Dogs barked, then there were shots.

Tsiko grabbed Etienne by the arm and dragged him into his grandmother's longhouse. They peeked from the doorway at the band of warriors running into the village. There had to be at least twenty. All had painted faces and all carried muskets.

"Iroquois," Tsiko hissed. With his finger to his lips, he motioned Etienne to get down.

"How will we get out of here?" Etienne whispered, frozen in fear.

Then they heard Father Daniel's voice call out, "Receive baptism before it is too late."

The boys looked around the corner to see him hastening from building to building, calling on the Huron to be baptized. The boys pulled the Jesuit inside when he reached their doorway.

"You must hide," Tsiko told him.

"The Iroquois will kill you for sure," Etienne said, taking Father Daniel's arm.

The priest shook his head and yanked his arm back. "I must prepare my people," he said. "Fly to Sainte-Marie," he said as he ran out. "They must be warned."

The boys watched the Jesuit make his way back to the church, followed by a throng of women. They held their children out to him, wailing in despair.

The fierce yell of the Iroquois war-whoop rose again.

Etienne desperately hoped Tsiko would not drag him into battle. "What do we do?" he asked in a cracked voice.

Tsiko's grandmother made her way to the back door of the longhouse and gave instructions. The crowd of women, carrying babies with children clinging to hands and skirts, moved out and along the palisade wall.

Tsiko and Etienne ran to the doorway of the next longhouse. From there they watched Father Daniel immerse his handkerchief in a bowl of water. He shook it over those who crowded around. "Today we shall all be in Heaven," he said as the drops fell from the square of linen.

"I'm not going to Heaven today," Tsiko whispered.

Wide-eyed, Etienne nodded.

Fiery arrows shot across the sky. One fell at the foot of the palisade, setting the poles ablaze. Another landed on top in a flurry of sparks. The flames spread from one roof to another.

A burning post crashed. Another fell, striking a woman with a baby on her back.

The woman behind her put down her own child and rushed to her side. She rolled the woman over and undid the cradleboard straps. She lifted the cradle and baby, took her child's hand and ran for the opening into the forest. There was a loud bang. The woman arched her back as the shot hit her and she dropped the baby.

Etienne and Tsiko leaped across the glowing poles. The hot breath nearly strangled them. Etienne stumbled to his knees just as a shot rang out over his head. He picked up the cradleboard as Tsiko grabbed the child.

Another section of the burning palisade collapsed.

This time it fell backwards into the stream, encasing them in a wave of thick black smoke. "Stay in smoke," Tsiko said, pulling Etienne in his direction. They ran through the gap in the palisade wall, clutching the children, coughing and choking. The old man who had played with the boys took the cradle from his arms.

Etienne felt someone grab him.

It was Tsiko

Through the cloud of smoke, the trees beside the trail loomed tall and silent.

"Climb," Tsiko commanded from the base of a pine tree. "There will be scouts."

Etienne stared after the crowd of people making their way down the trail.

"Climb," Tsiko repeated, scrambling up the lower branches like rungs of a ladder.

Etienne followed, pulling himself through the dense, scratchy branches, his head throbbing from the heat. Thick coils of smoke wound and billowed around them, making their eyes sting. As they hid, they could see the shadows of intruders with raised tomahawks running through the village. Others moved about, torching anything that would burn.

Father Daniel, radiant in his vestments, confronted the raiding party. He raised his wooden cross and spoke.

The Iroquois stared at him in amazement. Then, with wide grins across their faces, they reached for their arrows and bent their bows.

Etienne closed his eyes so he wouldn't see the volley of arrows tear into the priest's robes, but the musket bang jolted them open. Tongues of flame illuminated the scene. The warriors rushed upon the fallen Jesuit with yells of triumph. They covered their hands in his blood and smeared it on their faces.

Etienne's heart pounded like a drum.

Fire engulfed the church. The warriors picked up the Jesuit's body and heaved it inside. The roar of the flames grew louder. The elm beside them screeched as its bark cracked. Etienne watched in horror as flames rushed up the tree.

"Jump," Tsiko commanded. "Like a squirrel."

Sick and dizzy, Etienne reached out for a branch, following Tsiko. He swung again and again. The trees were getting smaller, but he had no idea where he was. He could no longer see Tsiko but dared not call out.

For a moment, he saw himself laid out for burial like Jacques Douart. His mother kneeled at his side, weeping. But he shook the thought away. He vowed she would see him again alive.

Voices seemed to travel from tree to tree. Out of exhaustion, Etienne lost his grip. He landed with a bump and rolled down a hill. As he crawled through the brush, the thorns and nettles scratched his body, and as he scrambled to his feet, he was surprised he wasn't hurt.

He made it to the river bank. Even there the air held the heat of the blazing village.

Several canoes came to a stop and warriors jumped out.

Etienne fell to his knees He could run no longer, and he hung his head, awaiting his fate. As the warriors rushed towards him, he passed out.

SEVENTEEN

The Burial

Etienne sat facing the doctor with a blanket draped about his shoulders. The black smoke that had filled his lungs had scorched his throat. He coughed several times.

Father Bressani hurried to the bucket and dipped in the ladle. He stood with his hand on Etienne's shoulder as the boy drank.

"Thomas and I took to the trees," Etienne said hoarsely. "Then we saw..." He tried to speak of the fate of Father Daniel, but he choked with the emotion.

"Thank the Lord both of you are safe," Master Gendron said. "Others were not so lucky."

"Both of us?" Etienne repeated as he looked up at the doctor. "Thomas is safe?"

The doctor nodded.

Etienne buried his head in the folds of the blanket in relief.

In the loft that night, he opened the embossed case with the mirrored lid. A crust of dried blood sat at the corner of his mouth. He wet his finger, touched it, then put his finger back in his mouth. The taste frightened him. He pushed his fists into his red-rimmed, bloodshot eyes in an effort to block out the memory of Father Daniel's fate.

Ambroise stomped in carrying a candle. He kneeled by his bed and mumbled. "I ask for the grace to persevere till death as a helper of these holy missionaries."

Etienne stirred at his words.

"You are not asleep?' Ambroise asked, holding the candle high.

"No," Etienne said, turning his face away from the light.

"The Lord protects those in times of trouble," the cook said. He made the sign of the cross. "I will pray for your peace of mind."

Etienne tried to listen, but the words of the prayer slipped past him. He remembered how Brother Douart had looked at the Hurons in disdain and had taken pleasure in their discomfort. The longhouse was hardly a stone's throw away, but Father Mesquin never saw those that lived in it as real people with real families.

"I must look in on the chickens," Etienne choked out as he bolted from his bed.

In the poultry house, the Houdans huddled under their wings. Sleeping pigeons balanced along the roost. Ignoring the sour smell of dust and dung, Etienne flung himself onto a nesting mound of grass and sobbed. That night, he slept with the chickens.

* * *

It should have been the kind of morning when Etienne

could fill his lungs with the fragrance of sweetgrass, but he raised his matted head to a smoke-filled sky. Even though he was still coughing, he knew he had to get to the hospital. The doctor would need plenty of assistance.

Survivors were streaming through the gate, and small cone-shaped tents covered the grassy common. Those who lived told how the Huron warriors had returned and the fighting had grown fierce. But their numbers had been no match for the Iroquois, who had hunted the woods all the next day. Cries of infants gave away mothers unable to travel far. The Iroquois had marched their prisoners off to their village, but many had died along the way. The grey, gritty air was thick with worry.

Fathers Rageuneau and Bressani went from bed to bed in the hospital as Etienne filled gourd cups with root tea. The Jesuits wished to compile a list of the dead, but no one would give names.

"They believe if they say the deceased's name, it will stop their soul from going to heaven," Father Bressani told the Father Superior with a great sigh.

"Their souls must journey towards the setting sun," the doctor added from across the room. The shadows in the room intensified the lines of fatigue across his forehead.

"I want to help bury the dead," Etienne said to the doctor as the priests walked past.

Both Jesuits blinked at him in surprise.

"Why would you want to do that?" Father Bressani asked.

"The people in the village were my friends," he said.

"They will need help."

Father Bressani moved closer to the doctor. "They do not bury their people in the same manner," he said in a whisper.

"He needs to come to terms with the matter," the doctor replied. "We cannot allow the blackness of what he has witnessed to smoulder. It must be dampened with good deeds."

Father Rageuneau nodded and beckoned Etienne to him. "First they will bury the infants along the village paths," he said in a low voice. "They hope their spirit will enter a passing woman to be reborn." The Father Superior waited for Etienne's reaction.

"Do the others go into the ground?" Etienne asked, not questioning the practice.

"No, they carry the bodies to an isolated place," Father Bressani said. He shook his head in wonder. "After their family has gazed upon them, they cover them."

"And then they bury them?" Etienne asked.

"They do not," the Father Superior said in a sad, low voice. "They leave the bodies to the elements, allowing the bones to be cleaned."

"But Thomas said they would be buried," Etienne whispered.

"They will be, but much later," Father Rageuneau said, fingering the wooden cross on his chest. "On the Feast of the Dead, the bones are put in caskets of bark." He sighed. "Then they are placed in a large pit." He shook his head. "They believe when the bones mingle, the souls of their family will meet again."

Etienne stared down at his feet. All the bones mingled together. Tsiko's mother lay in the churchyard at the mission. Now he knew why her brothers were so displeased. They believed there was no chance of ever meeting their sister again.

"It is not a pleasant sight, from what I have been told," Father Rageuneau concluded. He sighed. "But if your curiosity is greater than the telling, feel free to go."

"But no one is allowed to leave the mission," Father Bressani protested. "You gave that order yourself."

"Not even the Iroquois will attack a funeral procession," Father Rageuneau replied. He paused in the doorway and looked back at Etienne. "If it is too much for you, return with those who bring Father Daniel to St. Joseph. But you had better tell Master Broulet where you are going," he added. "He complains of your thrashing about with bad dreams."

There was little left of Teanaustaye when Etienne and Tsiko arrived. The blackened branches of the burned longhouses moved in the breeze like desperate fingers. Gusts of wind made the embers glow, as if the village gave out its very last heart beats.

The smouldering ashes warmed their moccasins. Charred bodies lay everywhere. Etienne retched on the burned, black grass. His next wave of nausea came at the sight of several bodies in a heap. He willed himself to be brave like the Hurons as he helped to lift the blanket-wrapped corpses into the canoes.

Etienne picked up his paddle and took his place at the stern. Tsiko waited in the bow.

Soo-Taie sat as still as stone, her white knuckles

gripping the side of the canoe. The folds of the beautifully beaded cloak draped about her shoulders did not soften her look. With the death of Tsiko's grandmother, she was now head of the Deer clan.

Etienne could feel the hurt in her heart.

The procession moved down the river, paddles in perfect unison. An enormous colony of swallows burst from the tops of the trees. They twisted and turned as they wheeled across the sky. Within minutes, a second flock burst out, then another and another, until the sky filled with whirling birds. Then, as if by signal, a large number of them suddenly separated from the others and flew down the long stretch of the riverbed. Making a wide turn, they dipped and dove, then disappeared. The rest of the birds followed the canoes a short way downriver, then flew behind the trees and disappeared into the clouds. It was as if they had come to say goodbye.

They paddled to a small island with a beach of stones. Many trees covered the grassy hill. An old Huron with flowing white hair stood at the top, holding his arms to the sun. Bright yellow birds, darting in and about the branches, seemed somehow out of place.

Etienne helped carry their dead up the grassy mound. They placed the bodies on platforms in and around the trees and covered them with beaver skins. A low whispering sound came from the wind playing about the clothes and trinkets of the dead. Everyone placed a hand on the tree trunks and wished the dead a safe journey to the land of the sun.

The sun tipped the treetops with gold and the wavelets

with silver as Etienne waited on the beach, tossing stones into the water. A perfectly round pebble caught his eye. He picked it up to throw but instead put it into the small tin at his side.

EIGHTEEN
Feather-at-My-Feet

"We are but forty Frenchmen in the middle of an infidel nation," Father Rageuneau said after evening grace. "It is from God alone that we wait for reward."

"I'm not planning to wait for that reward," Etienne whispered to Nicholas in the kitchen.

"No one is going to get out of here," Nicholas said. He gave Etienne a pleading look. "If we stay, we will surely die." His eyes filled with tears. "If we leave, we break our vows and lose grace."

Etienne straightened his shoulders and shivered. His mouth was too dry to speak. He had already seen what the Iroquois could do. His heart filled with dread, even though the sun shone and the birds sang. With a heavy heart, he went to the loft to think about his future.

*　　*　　*

Each morning, he hoped it would be the day his two voyageur friends returned. It was time for him to think about heading home. Twelve small circular moons decorated the thin headboard of his bed. Etienne rinsed Pierre's red sash in the river, thinking how happy he would be to hear how it had helped save Tsiko.

*   *   *

At the apothecary, Etienne handed the leather apron to the doctor, who took it from him and examined the workmanship. "Where did you get this?"

Etienne shrugged. "I brought it from Sillery."

"It was your father's," the doctor surmised.

"It is for you," was all Etienne said.

The doctor nodded in thanks and smiled as he tried it on.

The joy of giving the gift suddenly disappeared. Once Etienne left, there would be no more tramps in the forest for herbs. He would miss the comfortable silence of the priests at prayer, seeing the Huron women at work and watching the doctor as he made medicine.

*   *   *

Etienne raised himself on his elbows and listened to the heavy breathing of the men. He slid into his clothes and waited on the floor next to his bed.

Keeping his eyes on their sleeping forms, he pulled out the knitting from his bag and gave the wool a tug. Row by row, the little knots fell apart and the loops unravelled. He wound the coarse hairy wool into a crinkly ball. This he could give to Master Masson, the tailor. The wooden needles could go to Soo-Taie.

He smiled at the screech of the owl. It would be Tsiko. He could imitate the calls of all the birds except the chicken. He crept down the stairs.

In the hen house, Tsiko held out a bundle. "Tonight you wear this."

"It's for me?" Etienne asked as he unfolded a pair of soft, tanned deerskin breeches.

Tsiko nodded. He placed a necklace of shells in Etienne's hand. It was the one he had worn the first day they'd met.

The boys waited for the sentry to move away from his post. Without a sound, Tsiko manoeuvred the canoe through the weeds. Etienne could hardly contain his excitement. Tonight he would attend the Huron Council.

The encircling grove of giant pines reminded Etienne of the great cathedral his mother had talked of visiting as a girl. The smoke from the blaze in the centre hung amid the branches. Satouta stood in a patch of silver moonlight in front of the clearing. All pairs of dark eyes turned to them as they slid into place.

Watching Satouta's gestures and listening to the Huron words, Etienne understood what the council was hearing. Satouta mimed how Etienne had hunted beaver and built a fire to save his Huron brother. He told them how Etienne had called out to the Great Hawendio for help.

Satouta then explained to the warriors how Etienne's dreams had foretold the fires that destroyed his drum and the village. He told the men that Etienne had helped the children escape.

When his speech ended, the men in the circle grunted. Satouta approached Etienne. "Rise," he said. Etienne received the feather of a red-tailed hawk tied to the feather of a great-horned owl. Clapping Etienne on the back, Satouta called out. "Here is Feather-At-My-Feet."

The medicine man beat his rattle against the palm of his hand. Some men rose to their feet and formed a circle while others drummed. Tsiko seized Etienne's hand and pulled him into the circle. The drums changed their rhythm, and the line moved forward. As the thunder of the drums took over his body, Etienne shuffled his feet in time. With a swaying, rocking motion, the circle moved. The clouds seemed to shuffle to the rhythm as well, allowing the moon to break through. The ancient dance ended at sunrise with the laughing call of the loon.

Back at the hen-house, Etienne changed his clothes. He hid them, along with his feathers, in a nesting box just as the soldier on duty announced an arrival. Etienne scampered up the ladder to the rampart. The black dot on the horizon became a canoe, and the canoe had a painted eye.

NINETEEN
Trois Rivières

Etienne ran to Médard and flung his arms about his waist, but after a quick pat on the shoulder, the voyageur moved him aside and made his way to the gathering crowd. He appeared much older and very tired.

A murmur went up among the waiting crowd when they heard the news. The Iroquois had taken Pierre Leroux, the clerk.

"The Governor-General will be at Trois Rivières to reaffirm the French-Huron alliance," Father Bressani told them all at dinner. "A party of representatives from the mission must go to request protection. We need more soldiers and firearms. Monsieur des Groseilliers and anyone that wishes to trade will accompany us in one week's time."

"Is it safe to travel?"

"We cannot let those devils stop us."

"The soldiers must go as well."

"What if the Iroquois attack Sainte-Marie while we are gone?"

Everyone talked at once. Etienne's mind raced. That

night he told Tsiko what he had heard.

"Huron Council tells us," Tsiko said, "we will go to our Tobacco Brothers."

Etienne's heart sank at the thought of Tsiko leaving. "If you leave," he said, placing his hand on his friend's shoulder, "I will leave too."

"We will journey together," Tsiko said, "like brothers."

*   *   *

Etienne plucked a large feather from the black-necked goose hanging in the kitchen. He trimmed it with his knife until the quill point was as fine and sharp as Soo-Taie's needle. When Tsiko entered the apothecary, Etienne was sitting at the doctor's table, copying words from one sheet of parchment to another.

Tsiko pretended not to be interested.

Etienne replaced the quill in the ink bottle and sat back in pride. "There," he said. "Now I will be able to sing Father Brébeuf's song too."

Tsiko's eyes narrowed as he approached. "You will not have time to learn his song," he said. "Father Brebeuf needs many weeks to teach you the words."

"I don't need anyone to teach me the words," Etienne replied. He tapped the paper with his fingers. "I have the words here."

Tsiko snatched up the paper and studied it.

"You've got it upside down," Etienne said. He took the paper and fixed it to a peg on the wall. "Give me one of your arrows," he said.

Tsiko, overcome with curiosity, removed an arrow from his quill and handed it over.

"You know the song best," Etienne said. "You can tell me if it is right." Using the stone tip, Etienne pointed to each word as he said it out loud.

Tsiko listened in amazement.

"Did I get it right?" asked Etienne.

Tsiko nodded. He stepped closer and peered at the lettering in front of him.

"The marks look like animal tracks," he said. He pointed to the "s" at the end of the first word, "just like a snake."

"Yes!" Etienne said with enthusiasm. "You're right! And since you know the words of the song so well, you can figure the rest of it out."

Tsiko's eyes went small. "How do you know this?" he asked.

"My mother taught me," Etienne said. "By the time I was five, I knew all the letters."

Tsiko shot a nervous look over his shoulder. "Only Black Robes read," he said.

"The doctor can read," Etienne said, "and he's not a Black Robe." He placed his hand on Tsiko's shoulder. "You can learn too." He pulled Tsiko closer to the paper on the wall. "You say the words, while I point."

After three repetitions, Etienne handed the arrow back to Tsiko, and both of them were smiling.

* * *

Etienne waited for Nicholas by the well. He removed his

fur vest and handed it to the carpenter's apprentice. "Try this on," he said.

Nicholas reached for it eagerly.

"You can keep it," Etienne said in a low voice.

Nicholas looked up in surprise. "But you will need it for this winter."

"I will not be here for the winter," Etienne whispered, putting his finger to his lip.

"Where will you go?" Nicholas asked.

"I will find a home," Etienne said with a catch in his throat.

A look of fear crossed Nicholas's face. "What about your duty to God?"

"Let me worry about that," Etienne said. He picked up his bucket and strolled away. He didn't dare share the details of his plans with Nicholas. He knew the boy would be duty-bound to tell the Jesuits everything he knew if questioned, and he needed to keep his departure a secret.

Tsiko and Etienne planned to travel to the first trading post before the group from Sainte-Marie. Tsiko would continue on his journey to the Tobacco People. Etienne would hide until Médard was ready to take him on to Trois Rivières.

*   *   *

"You take," Satouta said to Etienne in the longhouse. He handed the boy a small black bundle. The beaver pelts glistened in the glow of the fire.

Etienne didn't know what to say. This gift was unexpected,

and he had nothing to give in return. He put his hand on his hip, touching the tin at his side. Then he remembered the little round stone. He pulled it out and pressed it into Satouta's copper palm. "You take this," he said.

The warrior looked down at it in surprise.

"It's from the shore of your sacred place," Etienne said. "It will remind you of your village."

Satouta clenched it in his fist and nodded.

*   *   *

Everyone had busied themselves preparing for the journey. Soo-Taie threaded thin strips of meat onto branches and smoked them over the fire. The children filled woven sacks with beechnuts, black walnuts and acorns.

A sheathed knife lay across the blanketed poles at the bottom of Tsiko's canoe, along with two harpoons and a fishing-net. There were baskets of corn and makuks of brown sugar. Tsiko also had a stack of beaver pelts tucked in the bow.

Etienne wore his deerskin leggings and eagle feather. His other clothes and belongings were in the drawstring sack. At midnight, their little canoe scooted through the reedy swamp like a beaver. The yellow-eyed owl was their only witness. Etienne said a silent goodbye.

Soon the black, choppy waves slapped against the sides of the white bark. At the river's bend, Tsiko emptied the contents of a small drawstring pouch into the water.

Etienne looked down. "What was that?"

"Beaver bones," Tsiko replied. "They must always return to the river."

The first portage, through the cedars and down the rolling hills in the moonlight, would end at sunrise. They stopped their journey on foot at the bank of the next river. While Etienne collected wood, Tsiko plunged his hands into the water and came up with a large, gaping fish.

As they ate, Etienne couldn't help wondering about the fate of those who would stay to pray at Sainte-Marie.

TWENTY

Attack

Etienne returned to the routine of the journey with ease. When they weren't paddling, they staggered beneath the weight of their packs as they carried the canoe across the many portages. They carried their vessel across meadows and through forests. At times the trees were so dense all they had to follow was a thin line of dirt.

Day after day they cut silently through the green water. A silver coated lynx with tufts of hair on its ears crept along a rocky ledge at their side. As its short black-tipped tail disappeared into the underbrush, Etienne wondered what message it carried.

One afternoon, they passed a line of waterfalls with a rainbow at the foot. They paddled their way between the jagged rocks of the crooked river. Their little canoe picked up speed, and soon there seemed to be hundreds of rocks poking out of the water. The thunder of rapids roared ahead.

Etienne gazed anxiously ahead. "We won't make it!" he yelled as the spinning eddies snatched at their paddles. "We'll be dashed to pieces!" he screamed.

The waves lashed and smashed the bow of the leaping canoe. Etienne closed his eyes and held his breath. Suddenly they found themselves in a pool of deep, clear water, circling in an eddy. Their little canoe had shot across the rapids like a tiny stick.

Tsiko raised his paddle above his head and yelled in triumph. Etienne sat gasping in relief. He turned his eyes upward and gave thanks to the gods.

The journey filled Etienne with memories of the previous year, setting out into the wilderness for the first time. No longer the same young boy who had left, he had learned how to be a helper, a hunter, a healer and a hero. He knew he was ready to face his distant, brooding father.

They approached an area that Etienne recognized from the year before, but a strange gurgling sound came from the creek bed he had once walked with Médard. Yellow, muddy water carried matted masses of sticks and grass. "Something must have happened to the beaver pond," he told Tsiko.

"No time to look," Tsiko warned. "Eyes and ears are everywhere."

Etienne thought about how the Huron didn't really hunt the beaver so much as farmed them, as they did the land. They kept track of the lodges and knew the number of old and newly born in each. They feasted on their meat, made use of their fur, tail and claws. Tsiko's people even returned their bones to the river instead of giving them to their dogs.

The silver-tipped birch trees soon became few and far between. Etienne's mind drifted with the smell of pine that floated across the water. He could still see the surprise in Soo-Taie's deep brown eyes when he'd handed her the scissors. He remembered watching her pull porcupine quills for her designs.

The countryside of fallen trees, marsh and brush gave way to the cold, forbidding mountains. *Is this how I will find them at home?* he wondered.

That night the boys moored at an outcrop of rocks just before the river narrowed and turned. They lifted the canoe from the water to examine it.

"It needs a patch," Etienne said, sticking his finger into a small tear at the side. He looked around for a birch tree, but there were none in sight.

Tsiko pulled a long roll of birch bark from his deerskin pouch and a coil of *wattape*, a kind of string made by his people. "This will do," he said, cutting a piece from each.

Etienne helped remove the torn stitching and patch the frayed canoe.

Tsiko scraped a wad of resin from a nearby pine with a stick, heated it in the fire and sealed the patch.

A duck flew from the reeds at the side of the river bank. Tsiko grabbed an arrow and let it fly.

"Will I ever learn to shoot that well?' Etienne wondered aloud as he waded out to retrieve the bird.

"Just shoot every day," Tsiko said with a shrug.

They built a fire in a dry, open spot. Tsiko held the duck to the sky in thanks. He plucked the feathers, put some of them into his pouch and gave the others to Etienne. Then he slit the duck down the middle and fixed each half to a roasting stick. Etienne tossed a handful of beechnuts into the coals. As the heat cracked them open, the boys enjoyed the small, tasty treasures.

As they ate, Etienne thought about the forest of brilliant green pine and golden birch. The land teemed with birds, animals, berries and nuts. The cold, crystal clear lakes and rivers were full of fish. These forests had everything anyone could want. And yet his father cut the trees down to make room for his fields. More farmers would come. Would there be enough forest left for the Hurons or the Iroquois?

The sharp sound of a crow drifted through the trees. Tsiko stopped eating when the sound of an owl came from across the water. His eyebrows furrowed and his forehead creased with a frown. "Something isn't right," he said. "Crows know if there is an owl in the forest. The owl is the crow's worst enemy."

He doused the fire and gestured for Etienne to get down. Like snakes they moved into the tall grass of the river bank to investigate. A disturbed bird whirred past them, so close that Etienne felt the flutter of its wings on his face. It shot across the river and disappeared in the evening light.

Tsiko scanned the water. "Look," he said, pointing to the shore on other side. "Beside the rock, I saw a splash of a paddle."

Etienne could hardly believe his friend saw anything at all, especially so far away in the dusk.

Tsiko cupped his mouth and made his own owl sound. A moment later, a similar sound came back. "I thought so," he said. "Someone is signaling."

"At least they are on the other side," Etienne said.

No sooner had the words come out of his mouth than a canoe shot out from the opposite river bank, heading right for them. Moments later, it turned. The boys watched the warrior paddle downstream to where a second canoe joined him.

"They're Iroquois scouts," Tsiko whispered.

Etienne felt a cold chill go up his spine when he saw the large war canoe carrying painted warriors follow the scouts down river.

The French boy and the Huron youth exchanged glances. There was no doubt in their minds that the Iroquois were planning an ambush.

"We have to hide," Etienne said, trying to keep the panic out of his voice.

Tsiko nodded and pointed downstream. Where the river narrowed, a great willow had fallen from the bank into the water. Its mass of tangled roots spread out in all directions. The tree had not been down long. The trailing branches and leaves were still green.

"Good idea," Etienne said.

"I'll check the canoe," Tsiko said as he slipped into the water.

Etienne went back for their things. Their canoe rested exactly as they had left it. As far as they could see, nothing had been disturbed.

The boys waited until the night clouds dimmed the sky then paddled to where the willow rested. They hid their canoe in the density of its roots, climbed into the boughs and flattened themselves against the trunk.

The only sign they left was their cold fire pit.

The Iroquois crossed the water like shadows, searching the woods. One held a burning roll of birch bark above his head as he peered in the direction of the boys. In their willow branch cavern, perched above the dark water, the boys didn't stir. The faces of his mother and father floated before Etienne's eyes. He was halfway home. Would he ever make it there?

*   *   *

When the sun rose, the boys watched the first of the Mission's two canoes come into view. Father Bressani rode with the Huron traders beside Satouta in the front. The French soldiers followed a short distance behind. Médard, assisted by Louise Gaubert, paddled his birch-bark alongside.

The first canoe anchored by the same rocky outcrop that the boys had used the day before.

"Why are they stopping?" Etienne whispered.

"Traders must put on face," Tsiko answered, easing down the trunk.

Etienne knew the Huron painted their faces and greased their hair to make themselves presentable, but there were Iroquois about. "They have to be warned," he said.

"You tell Father Bressani," Tsiko said, as he waded into the water. "I'll warn the others."

He swam to the rocks as silently as a fish, his long black ponytail floating behind him.

Etienne followed in the canoe.

Father Bressani stood on a rock, wringing out his robes.

"You are in danger," Etienne called out to the Jesuit.

The surprised Jesuit regarded the boy with a puzzled expression. "Why are you here?" he asked. "Does Father Rageuneau know you have left the mission?"

"You have to come with me," Etienne insisted. "The Iroquois are around the bend."

"Iroquois have never been on this part of the St. Lawrence," scoffed the Jesuit. "In all my years as a missionary..." he said, just as a war-whoop erupted across the water.

Tsiko flashed from the water like a trout eating a fly. He grabbed the hem of the priest's cassock and yanked him down.

Father Bressani floundered about in the river

Etienne dragged the confused Jesuit into the canoe. Tsiko leaped in behind. The boys dipped their paddles deep and sent the canoe surging forward to the shelter of the fallen tree.

Tsiko's warning gave the Huron time to remove their caskets of corn and nuts, bundles of fur and other trade goods from the canoe and prepare for battle.

The Iroquois scouts appeared in the narrows

The Hurons paddled fiercely. They rammed the Iroquois canoes and sent them spinning.

One scout dove into the water as his canoe swung up onto the rocks. The other leaped into the Huron canoe brandishing his tomahawk. A Huron warrior raised a gleaming knife. The Huron threw the attacker's body over the side.

Shots rang out as the French soldiers moved up river. The Huron canoe moved deftly around the warcraft, forcing it towards the soldiers, just as a second Iroquois warcraft, hidden round the bend, made its appearance.

Etienne, Tsiko and Father Bressani watched its arrival through their screen of branches.

"We'll have to go by land," Tsiko said from their branchy cover. "We can rejoin the river around the bend."

Etienne agreed. If they could get past the Iroquois, the trading post was only leagues away,

"Take Father Bressani as prisoner," Etienne directed. "If you are seen, they will think you are Iroquois."

The priest nodded.

"I will bring the canoe."

Tsiko bound the priest's hands behind his back with strips of willow. He led the way into the forest. The priest followed without a word.

There was just enough space for Etienne to push their canoe beneath the toppled tree trunk. He had to make it look abandoned as it floated downstream. If spotted, he would be killed or captured. He swallowed his fear and placed a water-soaked log, the same thickness and length as his body, inside, next to the paddles. If an Iroquois bullet cut through the side, he wanted it in the log, not his body.

Etienne slipped into the dark water, hiding alongside the canoe, and watched the battle with nose and eyes just above the surface. The canoe of French soldiers fought directly across from the Iroquois craft. The deafening discharge of muskets close by made him turn. Someone was shooting from the rocks.

Médard stood on the rocks, in the open, firing at the Iroquois from behind. Louise Gaubert, barricaded by the trading goods, aimed for their hull. The enemy war-canoe began to sink.

Etienne let the current carry him and his canoe past the second pair of battling craft. Wounded Hurons and Iroquois dropped into the water amid the smoke that drifted to shore.

*   *   *

"I hear something," Tsiko whispered as he and Father Bressani emerged from the trees near the point. They stopped, letting their bodies blend into the dense foliage. The way to the river seemed impossible.

A wet Iroquois climbed the rocky bank to the grassy verge. Tsiko pulled back his bow and shot him in the chest. He cut Father Bressani's bonds so he could lift his skirts to run.

The small birch-bark canoe shone silver in the late afternoon sun as it floated into a marshy cove. Something beside it flashed like fish at play.

Tsiko placed his hands to his mouth and made the sound of an owl.

Etienne rose to an upright position. He tossed the log over the side and climbed in.

They paddled quickly away from the din of shouts and shooting, heading downstream to the trading post.

*   *   *

The passageway of white, red and green blankets tossed over poles along the riverbank signalled the approach to the trading post. Its stern-faced wooden church rose above the warehouse, tents and log buildings. The muggy air held the stench of fish, smoke and garbage. Here, the flies were fatter.

Médard des Groseilliers, Louis Gaubert and the Hurons arrived much later, tired and bloodied. They had taken Iroquois prisoners. Father Bressani, Tsiko and Etienne watched them force their attackers to kneel before the cross.

A beardless man in a threadbare coat also watched. His greasy hair smeared the crown of his head in an attempt to hide his baldness. When he smiled at the discomfort of the Iroquois, Etienne recognized the pock-marked face, scarred nostril and broken, blackened teeth.

TWENTY-ONE

The Trader

Etienne moved behind Tsiko. The trader approached them with a smile. "We meet again," he said to Etienne.

"I don't think we have met before," Etienne replied.

"You have your mother's eyes," the man said. "Days ago, I spoke with your father."

Etienne was desperate to ask what they had spoken about. He wanted to know about the farm, the animals, and most of all about his mother, but he couldn't with Father Bressani so close.

"Was he alone?" Etienne asked.

The trader scratched his chin in thought. "Come to think of it, there was a boy with him," he said. "He looked about your age."

"You see, you are mistaken," Etienne said with feigned indignation. "It must have been another man and his son that you met."

"But I know François Chouart well," the trader continued. "I hoped he'd invite me to his house for a meal, as he did once before. His wife is a fine cook."

Father Bressani moved closer.

"Matter of fact," the trader continued, "he said he would have done, but his wife was feeling poorly." He looked directly into Etienne's eyes, waiting for a reaction.

Tsiko stepped between them. "You want to make a good trade?" he asked. He took the man by the arm and led him away. "My brothers brought many things to the trading post."

"We'll meet again," the trader said, shooting a glance over his shoulder.

Etienne went to his small wooden bed in the bunkhouse. He drew out the silver mirrored case and opened it. "Our parents live within us," his mother often said. He used to think she meant like ghosts, but when he looked into the mirror, he understood. He did have his mother's eyes. He stroked the mirror with a finger, imagining it was her face looking back at him. His throat felt tight at the thought of her not being well.

A creak in the plank floor interrupted his thoughts. Tsiko stood in front of him.

"This trader," he said in a low voice, "do you know him?"

Etienne stared at his feet.

"I watched the way he looked at you," Tsiko continued. "He knew you."

Etienne still did not reply.

"You met him some other time?" Tsiko asked, crossing his arms in front of him.

Etienne nodded. "Yes," he said, "a long, long time ago."

Tsiko touched the tomahawk at his waist. "Enemy?"

Etienne shook his head. "No," he said, "my father brought him home. My mother cooked for him, and he told us stories."

Tsiko's brow furrowed. "I don't understand," he said.

"He knew me by a different name," Etienne said, snapping the mirrored case shut.

"What other name?" Tsiko asked in harsh whisper.

"My mother's name is Marie Catharine Chouart," Etienne said as he stood.

Tsiko's eyes widened, but, before he could protest, Etienne put his fingers to his friend's lips. "I can say her name out loud," he said, "because she is not dead, nor is my father."

Etienne watched the truth dawn on his friend.

"Then he really saw your father," Tsiko said. He stamped his feet in anger. "Why did you keep this great secret?" But before Etienne could explain, Tsiko stormed out of the room.

Etienne knew he should have told Tsiko the truth long before, but he felt foolish admitting he was nothing but a runaway. He pulled the drawstring bag out from under his bunk and put the mirror back. His fingers touched the skin bundle, the other secret he had kept hidden for so long.

He found Tsiko sitting beside his canoe along the water's edge. He handed the bundle to the sulking Huron boy. "This is to repair the crack in our friendship," Etienne said.

The Huron boy took the bundle. His eyes opened wide at the surprise of seeing his grandmother's yellow-feathered drum.

"Sometimes when you give a friend a secret," Etienne said, "it burns a hole in their heart." He slumped down beside his friend. "I ran away for adventure."

Tsiko carefully rewrapped the drum and placed it on his lap. "Iroquois make plenty adventure."

They erupted into laughter.

"You will return to your parents now?" When Etienne nodded, Tsiko removed his pouch and gave it to Etienne. "May the Lord watch over you," he said.

"May Hawendio keep your paddle strong," Etienne replied, accepting the gift. "You could come back with me," he said with a smile, "and help to feed the chickens."

"I prefer warbird over chicken," the Huron boy said, thumping his chest and smiling.

Etienne heard the swish of Father Bressani's cassock from behind. The Jesuit placed his gnarled hand on Etienne's shoulder. "My prayers have been answered," he said. "You are not going to continue the journey to the Tobacco Nations with Thomas after all."

Etienne took a deep breath. "I won't be returning to Sainte-Marie with you, either."

"You prefer to travel back with Samuel-Satouta?" Father Bressani asked.

"I am going home," Etienne said. His eyes glistened as he spoke. "My real name is Etienne Chouart," he blurted out. "My parents, Marie and François Chouart, live near Kebec. I am not an orphan." He let out a great sigh, the burden of his lie finally lifted.

The priest regarded him for a second as if expecting further explanation. But Etienne had no more to say.

"Well then," Father Bressani said, letting out a deep breath, "you must be dismissed from your duties." Shaking his head in disbelief, he turned and walked away. But he stopped and looked back.

Their eyes met. Etienne braced himself for a tongue-lashing. But the priest's face did not show anger. He flashed a tired smile and made the sign of the cross. His last words were, "I thank thee, Heavenly Father, for your great mercy to me, Etienne and Thomas. Hold them forever in thy precious keeping."

Etienne felt his face grow hot.

That night his hands trembled as he packed his few remaining things.

TWENTY-TWO

Home

Silver poplars sparkled among the maple trees. As the canoe approached the hillsides of fruit trees, Etienne noticed a new dyke along the north bank of the river.

"Well, my little one," Médard said, holding his paddle to shore, "back to the beginning."

"Will you pass this way again?" Etienne asked, hauling his packs from the canoe.

The voyageur smiled. "*Mais oui*," he said, shaking the boy's hand. "I will see you again."

Etienne walked along a roadside lined with golden ragweed, bull rushes and clumps of purple pokers. In the dust were signs that a snake had passed this way and he could see the tiny prints of a raccoon. He stopped to examine a patch of yellow flowers. *What name do they go by?* he wondered. *What is their medicine?* He decided he would keep a book of plants, like the doctor.

Fluffy white clouds with flat grey bottoms moved across the bright blue sky. The breeze brought him the smell of sheep, pigs and cattle.

His heart pounded at a sudden thought that dropped

into his heart like a stone. *What if they are no longer here?* He raced down the slope.

The sound of an axe echoed across the land. Etienne stared at the lone figure in the field. The axe hit a rock, and a loud voice peppered the air with curses. "That's my father," Etienne cried out, feeling his blood rush to his face, as he ran towards the house.

Etienne stopped at the small kitchen window to peer inside. The fire in the grate was small. His mother bustled about the kitchen, setting out three bowls and spoons. Then, as if she sensed something in the breeze, like a doe, she looked up with eyes that had lost their sparkle.

Etienne dropped his packs and pushed open the door. "*Me voici, mère,*" he said. "It's me."

Marie Chouart's hands went first to her mouth. Then her arms shot out. She looked at Etienne in surprise then pulled him to her.

Sobbing, she broke her embrace, placed her hands on his shoulders and pushed him down onto the wooden bench. "Sit down," she said, "I want to look at you." She touched one cheek then the other. "Your skin is so dark," she said, her eyes searching his face

"It's from the sun," was all he could think to say.

The boy entered the house first. Etienne's glance took in his clean linen shirt and woollen breeches. The boy's face, no longer gaunt, looked round and full.

Etienne's father followed.

François Chouart stopped short. He ran his hand down his greying beard. Etienne watched his father's face. He was so very pale, with great shadows under his eyes. Would it change like the sky into a cloud of thunder, black with anger?

"You are so rough and brown. I would have taken you for a savage," was all he said.

The orphan boy could only stare.

The steam rising from the iron pot caught Etienne's eye. He turned to it. His mother, seeing the hunger in his eyes, quickly filled a bowl. "Here," she said, pressing it into his hands and guiding him to the table.

The first mouthful burned his lips, but he was so hungry, he kept on. He hadn't tasted food this good in a long time. When finished, he held on to the bowl, as tense as an animal and waited.

Without speaking, his father walked back outside. He retrieved the bundles Etienne had left on the ground and carried them into the farmhouse.

Etienne put down his bowl and left the table. He opened the drawstring bag and handed his mother a small square birch-bark basket. "A few grains will go well in your pumpkin loaf," he said with a smile. "You can add dried berries too."

She looked up at him in surprise.

"And the leaves of the raspberry bush make a very good tea," he added.

Her face broke into a wide smile.

"Fishing is a failure in Kebec," his father said unexpectedly, "and a bad year for crops."

Etienne untied the blanket around the bundle of furs. "These should help us this winter."

His father lifted the pack, weighing it in his mind.

Then he shook his head in wonder. "Longer than this winter," he said.

The silver case with the mirror Etienne handed back to the boy. "I've got a good story about a mirror," he said. Then he paused. "I've forgotten your name."

"I never told you," the boy said. "It is Thomas."

This time it was Etienne's turn to stare.

"Your mother blamed herself for your leaving," his father said, with an edge to his voice. "I would return to the house to find her with a spoon in her hand, staring off at the heavens."

"You took *my* place to serve God," Thomas said, hanging his head.

Etienne's heart softened. Although touched by their belief that he was so pious, he had to tell the truth.

"I ran off to find adventure," Etienne said. "You were right," he said. "Life at the mission..." he paused to search for the right words, "was not as one would expect."

"Is it true that fingers and toes freeze in the night?" Thomas asked.

"Which is why I have these," Etienne said pulling out the deerskin mittens and moccasins.

His mother gasped and took them to examine the work.

Etienne took off his cap, decorated with braids of animal hair, claws, paws and feathers, and handed it to his father.

"You have returned in time to save us from a dire winter," his father said.

"Not as dire as the one I had," Etienne replied.

To everyone's surprise, his father threw back his head and laughed out loud.

Etienne stared at him in relief. His father's mirth drained much of the anxiety from his heart. Tomorrow, Etienne would tell him about planting beans, corn and squash all together. He would explain how placing small fish in the soil would feed the young plants. There would be talk of hunting beaver, maple sugar and so much more. How shocked his mother would be to hear of how the voyageurs opened the flour bag and made a small hollow with their fist. After cracking an egg into the hole, along with a bit of river water, they mixed the dough with unwashed hands to make small flat cakes, which they baked by the fire.

"We must thank God for your safe arrival," his mother said. She pulled the family to their knees in front of the fire.

Etienne closed his eyes. He thanked God heartily then prayed that Tsiko would reach his Tobacco Brothers. He would miss the boy who had taught him how to keep his eyes open to all the little things that happened around him. Then he grinned. His friend would be able to use his yellow-feathered drum to celebrate his own safe arrival and for dancing under the moon with his new family.

Author's Note

The French Jesuits founded the great mission of Sainte-Marie in 1639. This important historical site was in the heart of the land of the Huron people. Written reports from Father Paul Rageuneau, Father Superior of the mission, provided the information about the priests, donnés and lay brothers. Father Francesco Bressani, Father Antoine Daniel and Father Jean de Brébeuf all served at the mission. The Huron Carol is a Christmas hymn written in 1643 by Father Jean de Brébeuf. Brother Jacques Douart, murdered in April 1648, lies in the tiny cemetery.

Ambroise Broulet, cook, Louis Gaubert, blacksmith, François Gendron, doctor and apothecary, Robert Le Coq, business manager, and Pierre Masson, tailor, all worked at the mission.

Voyageur Médard Chouart des Groseilliers was an *engagé* at Sainte-Marie from 1640 to 1646 before returning to live in Quebec. At the mission he acquired valuable experience necessary for his later travels of discovery.

The hostility and warfare between the Iroquois and the Huron is historical fact.

The Iroquois did indeed capture and kill Father Antoine Daniel and destroy the village of St. Joseph, known as Teanaustaye. Jesuits Jean de Brébeuf and Gabriel Lalemant later met with the same fate in March of 1649. Captured with hundreds of Hurons, the Iroquois tortured them to death. Those at the mission waited for a second attack, but it did not come. Eventually the Jesuits burned Sainte-Marie to the ground and abandoned it.

With the greater part of their tribe killed or in captivity, the remaining Huron escaped south and westward in 1649. The Huron divided into two groups. One group settled in Quebec, the others continued to migrate, eventually settling in Ohio. The Quebec Wyandots are direct descendants of the Midland Huron.

Even though the life of Etienne Chouart, my eleven-year-old *donné*, is fictional, young boys did apprentice at Sainte Marie. Christian Hurons lived in the longhouse at the mission, but Tsiko, Satouta, and Soo-Taie are not real people.

Today, one is able to stand in the midst of Sainte-Marie's replicated buildings and get a true sense of the age. Thanks goes to Paula Wheeler of Hillsdale (Teanaustaye), Jamie Hunter the curator of the Huronia Museum in Midland, Ontario, Professor John Steckley of Humber College, Toronto and the definitive work of Grace Lee Nute. Thanks also go to Anna Gemza, Marjorie Cripps, and Corinne McCorkle, my writing group, Brenda Julie, Susan Onn and Nancy Wannamaker, my avid readers.

Born in Niagara Falls, Ontario, Jennifer Maruno came from a book loving family.

Writing as Jennifer Travis, she produced award-winning educational materials for Ontario School Boards. After retirement as an elementary school principal, Jennifer published short stories for a variety of children's magazines in Canada, Britain and United States. She lives in Burlington, Ontario, with her husband.

Her first novel with Napoleon, *When the Cherry Blossoms Fell*, was published in 2009.